Knitting Patterns from Atlantis

Gerry Maguire Thompson

Zen Teabags Press, London

Category: humour/ literature/ fantasy

ISBN: 978-0-9559837-0-2

Copyright 2008 Gerry Maguire Thompson

First printed September 2008

Gerry Maguire Thompson has asserted his right to be identified as the author of this work under the Copyright, Designs and Patents Act 1988

Mackerel image on cover courtesy of Debby Mason

All rights reserved. No part of this publication may be reproduced, stored in a retrieval system, or transmitted in any form or by any means, electronic, mechanical, photocopying, recording or otherwise without the prior permission of the copyright owners

ABOUT THE AUTHOR

Gerry Maguire Thompson is an Irish comedian and author from Tipperary. His books have sold hundreds of thousands of copies in ten languages.

Other humorous titles by Gerry Maguire Thompson:

Astral Sex to Zen Teabags - a humorous encyclopedia of New Age jargon

Cats are from Venus, Dogs are from Mars - a parody of intimate human relationship

The Weekend Shaman, and other New Age types - an illustrated catalogue of charlatans, imposters and dodgy characters

Represented by Susan Mears Literary Agency:
http://sm.rwn.webreality.co.uk

www.gerrythompson.co.uk

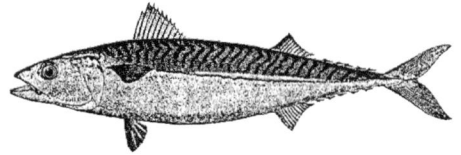

It was a fine, sunny August evening on the remote Irish isle of Inishower; that is to say, it was only raining a little. For the rain on Inishower had not stopped within living memory - nor did anyone expect it to; perhaps this was a factor in the island's almost exclusive population by writers, grass and sheep.

Inishower's annual literary festival, now in its twentieth year, was well under way. Tadgh McDadgh's harbourside *Café Bar de la Mer* was bursting to the gills with a riotous assembly of authors, celebrities, hacks, hangers-on and assorted poseurs from the island and from farther afield.

McDadgh's was the island's leading establishment for the synthesised pursuit of literary creation and alcoholic intake. He'd been running it for most of his life. Now a sprightly ninety-something, Tadgh had been a young man of eighteen when he received of one of the island's rare travelling bursaries, instigated to send local youngsters abroad every fifty years or so to find out how things literary were done in other parts of the world. That was in the nineteen twenties; the bursary committee had decided to send Tadgh to Paris due to rumours they'd heard of its influence at that time.

Tadgh, landing on his feet in Paris, quickly got drawn into the decadent literary society that dominated the bohemian fringes of Parisian society at that time. On his first day he happened to encounter a fellow by the name of James Joyce, whom Tadgh took to be a Jesuit priest - but who turned out to be a truly kindred spirit because like all Inishovians he hated everything to do with the Irish mainland. JJ was living in poverty and making a virtue of writing poems for mere pittances. He had chosen to eke out his existence in self-imposed exile here, from the mother country that he hated so bitterly yet seemed to make the setting for every novel, story, essay, poem, song, vignette, yarn or *bon-mot* that he created. The youthful and impressionable Tadgh was particularly taken with Joyce's stream-of-consciousness writing technique; JJ told him it was

1

inspired by the River Liffey in Dublin - a waterway which he loathed with a deep and bitter malice, yet which was the true central character in all his major works. Tadgh also learned that JJ's *Ulysses* had begun life as a proposed short story for the *Dubliners* series, but was rejected as too lightweight by the publisher. This was subsequently expanded by JJ into the longest and most successful book ever about the events of one day - purely in revenge against the rejection. Still stung by the event, JJ then went on to write *Finnegan's Wake*, carrying the same writing principles still further, drawing even greater critical acclaim, and making the publisher even more sorry that he'd turned down the earlier work. Tadgh, an Inishovian through and through, instinctively sensed the possibilities for such a fluid approach to writing in the watery context of his island home. Tadgh and JJ whiled away many happy hours at the *Café d'Hibernie*, drinking Irish coffees and talking together of things damp and moist.

Unfortunately Tadgh's acquaintance with JJ was to be cut short by Norah Barnacle, the woman who was to stick eponymously to the great man like a limpet throughout his life. Overhearing some of their conversations Norah became intensely jealous of the young Tadgh, for whom she was convinced JJ harboured intense and unnatural carnal longings; and that was the end of their friendship. JJ, however, decided to introduce Tadgh to his close friend and patron Ezra Pound, who took Tadgh under his wing at his regular table at the *Café des Artistes Expatriotiques* on the south bank, and taught him much about experimental poetry, fascism, treason and the tenets of the Imagist school of coffee-drinking. Unfortunately this friendship too became untenable because of the rabid attentions of Pound's nasty little dog Canto, who seemed to resent Tadgh's presence and bit his ankles incessantly, producing scars which Tadgh would later display with pride.

Pound in turn took Tadgh to meet his friend and confidante Gertrude Stein, whose salon in Montmartre was a gathering place for avant-garde European artists and penniless American writers. Thus Tadgh suddenly found himself at the epicentre of the world of experimental art and letters. Gertrude took a keen interest in the young *ingénue*, and at her invitation he was able to enjoy croissants and *pain au chocolat* in the company of such luminaries as Picasso, Braque, Matisse and the intensely surreal Man Ray. Gertrude also procured his services to pose naked for an array of abstract impressionists, cubists, pointillists, primitivists and assorted voyeurs of her acquaintance. This naturally led to many instances of sexual awakening for the boy, and the acquisition of several obscure practices that would result in a lifelong association between chocolate, pleasure and pain. Furthermore, Gertrude privately revealed to him the intimate secrets of her own literary style and oeuvre - the application of the ideas of abstract art to writing, featuring unconventional prose, meaningless repetition and disdain for punctuation that no one else could see the point of. Unfortunately Gertrude's lifelong companion Alice B. Toklas, who suspected vestigial heterosexual tendencies in her partner, grew wildly jealous of the increasingly lusty and popular Tadgh, and forbade his visits.

Gertrude, then, introduced her protégé to F. Scott Fitzgerald, whom Tadgh thought sounded like a wealthy Irish nobleman. F. Scott's opening remark to Tadgh, however, was to enquire whether the young man could 'lend him ten bucks'. F. Scott had recently come to France because life was cheaper than in the States, yet had already racked up steep debts there. Tadgh was able to procure the requisite bucks through services speedily rendered using methods taught to him by Miss Stein, and the two men formed a symbiotic relationship that would prove fruitful for both of them. Tadgh became a reliable source of bundles of ten bucks, while F. Scott taught Tadgh much of the writerly importance of maintaining a playboy lifestyle despite total lack of financial wherewithal. Problems came, however, from F. Scott's wife Zelda, who grew insanely jealous of Tadgh. Zelda had twigged that F. Scott only wanted people around him to use as characters in his novels, and she was determined to be the only such person in his life. The Tadgh episode in F. Scott's affairs thus caused the first of many nervous breakdowns for Zelda, and so Tadgh had to keep away from him too.

F. Scott, however, was able to arrange for Tadgh to meet Ernest Hemingway when he dropped by one day at F. Scott's table at the *Café Plume de ma Tante* to refill his hip flask of bourbon. Tadgh and Ernest hit it off immediately, and this turned out to be the longest lasting and most influential of Tadgh's informal Parisian apprenticeships - mainly because Ernest never allowed any of his associates to get close enough for jealousy to become an issue. Ernest, in point of fact, considered F. Scott a bit of a lightweight in terms of decadence and debauchery, and undertook to show Tadgh what the lifestyle of a real writing man was all about. Tadgh quickly learned the skills of drinking, brawling, posturing and womanising, and steadily came to recognise hunting, shooting, fishing, bull-fighting and driving ambulances in war zones as key sources of literary inspiration. He also picked up much information about different kinds of coffee and their influence on writing, which would stand him in good stead later. Action-man Ernest was particularly fond of a robust Arabica, which he preferred to grow, pick, roast, grind and brew himself.

Now, half a dozen decades later on Inishower, Tadgh still stoutly reflected the influence of his time in Paris, and most notably that of Ernest H. He still wrote in very short sentences and believed that you had to physically do anything before you deserved to write about it - whether this involved going for a walk, picking a fight, womanising wildly, finding things to shoot, having multiple marriages or making a cup of tea. That was why Tadgh had originally become the local 'bad boy' upon his return from the extended bursary trip. Finding no bulls on the island, Tadgh had taken to naked wrestling with the biggest of the Inishower Damp-faced Merino rams that he could find, but had to refrain from killing it for fear of incurring the wrath of island knitters for weakening the island's genetic pool. His attempts to start a civil war on the island, in order to come to the rescue of whichever side turned out to be the underdog, also came to naught because of the islanders' apathy in all things unconnected to writing. And the biggest game fish that he could find to pit himself against were the six-inch speckled trout in the island's boggy streams.

Now though, Tadgh's age was holding him back, and he had calmed down a bit. But he still enjoyed doing strange things with chocolate, and still told terrific drinking-adventures-with-Hemingway stories that went down particularly well with male American visitors, while the occasional female would still turn up at his place from somewhere overseas demanding to be womanised, which was a bonus. And he still ran popular workshops every year on big game hunting as an approach to writer's block.

The other major effect of the early odyssey on Tadgh's life was his conclusion that sitting around in cafés was what produced great writers, particularly if the writing was mingled with rounds of gossiping, drinking copious amounts of coffee and alcohol, and procuring sexual liaisons. Immediately upon returning home, therefore. Tadgh decided that his life's work was to create a conducive setting for just such activities on the island. So from the outset McDadgh's sprawling hotel and bar was intimately furnished with tiny tables where you could fit one person, or two if they sat very close together, tightly arranged in true café style so that everyone could hear each other's business. Tadgh also provided an extensive sidewalk section along the wall away from the harbour, with a big canopy where putative authors could sit daydreaming and watch the rain fall over the shrouded green island while trying to write. On the approach road, Tadgh had sought to recreate the familiar atmosphere of the French boulevard with a line of brutally pollarded privet bushes. He even managed to develop a strain of coffee bean, Coffea Aquifolia, which could just about survive on Inishower.

This approach to providing a hotbed for literary creativity had worked, up to a point. Nowadays at McDadgh's there was always a quorum of plump Americans, each at his or her own habitual table, working at his or her plump manuscript, staring at the rain and indulging in plates of plump local mackerel and plump chips. But during the festival the place became the special haunt of youthful literary celebrities that were over from England looking for trouble - young Turks who were infatuated with Tadgh's literary connections and inspired by his association with fighting, bad behaviour and leading-edge literature. This was the only place they'd drink; for they thought of themselves as men of reckless and dangerous physical behaviour even though few had done anything more violent than topping a boiled egg. And they were here tonight.

2 The Naked Lunchbox

On this fine damp evening at McDadgh's, the tall but corpulent figure of Dr. Ulick O'Toole was moving through the crowd, clad in his best Inishower rainproof tweeds. He welcomed newcomers, greeted old friends, promised favours and exuded self-importance. For the island's literary festival was the brainchild and cherished creation of this one man.

Although Dr. O'Toole was never above using the occasion to further his dodgier lascivious personal ends, carnal desire was relegated to second place on this occasion as he basked in prestige as festival director and M.C. for the evening. Dr. O'Toole had planned tonight's event for the literary notoriety which he was sure it would bestow upon proceedings. It was to be a combined reading by the most pugnacious of those young Turks from across the water.

When it seemed that another body could not be squeezed into the heaving throng, Dr. O'Toole decided to start. He pushed his way to the front and raised his voice above the din in stentorian tones.

"Ladies and gentlemen, islanders and visitors," he said, as hush quickly fell. "It is with considerable pride that I now introduce the main item on tonight's bill of entertainment: indeed, a highlight of this year's festival programme. The young writers whom you are about to hear have caused a mighty stir on the international literary scene due to their fierce energy and audacious spirit. In their writing and lifestyle alike they display virile creative daring. They write like the devil, and may be forgiven for behaving that way too. Ladies and gentlemen, please welcome Brad Saltfish and the Bad Boys of Books."

The audience applauded with noticeable reserve as six male twenty-somethings slouched their way to the front of the crowd, clutching garishly bound volumes and exuding petulance in a display of consummate self-consciousness. Five wore sharp suits, their ties meticulously disarranged and shirts pulled out of trousers in a carefully cultivated statement of not giving a shit what anybody thought of how they dressed. Brad Saltfish, clearly the undisputed leader of the pack, displayed the most highly developed combination of slouch and swagger while sporting a costume of tight-fitting black leathers with several feet of heavy silver chain. The others created a phalanx behind him in an apparent hierarchy of ability to convey threatening nastiness.

Now facing the audience, Brad Saltfish quickly built up a convincing impression of holding himself back from doing physical violence to them, just for being there. Onlookers seated at the front few rows of tables grew uncomfortable and edged back in their chairs. But right at the front, one person reacted differently. Sally-Anne Peachley, a well-tanned young trans-Atlantic visitor who seemed to be on the verge of bursting out of the tight-fitting crimson dress that matched her choice of lipstick, immediately began to take an interest in Brad's leather-clad groin. To tell the truth, she had first pricked up her ears upon Dr. O'Toole's mention of the word 'virile', and her shapely bottom now seemed unable to be quite still on her chair.

Saltfish took things slowly, projecting a menacing silence as he paced to and fro. With his combination of black outfit, cultivated anguish and predatory manner, he exuded something of the ambience of a panther with a bad migraine.

"All right, pay attention," he rasped in measured, testosterone-laden tones. At that point he caught sight of Sally-Anne, and a compliant bulge appeared in the confines of his leather-bound crotch. He permitted himself the hint of a smile on one side of the face only, which came out as a twisted kind of sneer. Then he held up a sulphurous yellow paperback embossed with a black skull.

"I'm going to read from my autobiographical novel, *Don't Fuck with Me 'Cos I'm Really Angry*. It's about life and pain and the integrity of the artist. It's extremely good." He paused to work up more of a head of bitter resentment. Sally-Anne was still eyeing his nether regions. He left another gap to emphasise his integrity as an artist.

"Right," he went on. "This is from chapter five, *I'm Really Going to Smash your Face In*. It's about the key role of destructive energy in the life of the truly creative spirit. Here's how it goes." Another pause, more artistic integrity.

Saltfish appeared now to have established the slow, controlled and ultimately self-conscious mode which he desired. At this point, however, factors quite beyond his influence took over. To the audience, the first evidence of these was that Brad's face suddenly turned to ghostly white, before being illuminated by a vivid red flash that emanated from behind them. Almost immediately Brad felt the floor shift bodily under his feet, and then heard the sound of the blast. One hundred and twenty-six millilitres of blood drained more or less instantaneously from his up-till-that-point tumescent member. This was quickly followed by a radical involuntary contraction of the rectal colon that released into his leather pants a package of material which would otherwise have been delivered the following morning, upon consumption of his first black coffee and cigarette. Straight after that, a wave of water crashed against the window behind the audience - for the explosion had in fact occurred outside the bar on the harbour side - at which point Brad began to shake uncontrollably; and the shaking wouldn't stop for some forty-seven minutes.

The audience also experienced the building shake, felt the dull thump, and heard the water wash against the wall, followed by the sound of debris clattering onto the pub roof. Hard men like Corbel McLintol the builder and nosey parkers such as Finbar McFogarty were outside in a flash. Small splinters of wood were still falling out of the sky. The quayside was awash with seawater, and a succession of afterwaves splashed all round the harbour.

Sally-Anne Peachley seemed to lose all interest in Brad Saltfish's groin after that. The reading did not continue; there was too much for the crowd to talk about. The dry cleaners at home eventually did a good job on Brad's pants, but he never did get another erection in that particular pair.

3 Dr. Ulick's Feeling for Rain

Back in July, Dr. O'Toole had been on the last leg of his regular walk along the old bog road below the mountain on Inishower. It was a fine evening, with only a drizzle as fine and sheer as the silk stockings he had once bought for his now departed wife, the time he took the long trip over the sea and over to Dublin. That was when they were courting forty years ago; he had never been back there, and never wanted to go. Indeed, he hadn't left the island since.

To tell the truth, Ulick O'Toole's passion for doctoring had never lain in tending to physical ailments, and his heart was certainly not in the work of stitching up casualties. He had never derived fulfilment from doling out regular island medical care - lancing boils, applying poultices, removing foreign bodies inserted unnaturally into bodily cavities, and all that sort of thing. His heart was in Inishower's literary festival; and it was in the creative writing classes that he had run in the village library for as long as anyone could remember; and most of all it was in his self-appointed custodianship of the lore of the island, whose history he had rewritten at least thirty-nine times in as many years.

It was one of those perfectly still evenings when everything seemed just as it should be; the festival would be starting in a week or so, a new set of classes would begin, and meanwhile there was time to do more work on *The History*. Across the bogland in front of him, the distant form of Fishtail Mountain could just be seen through the misty rain. The thin cry of the curlew spiralled into the still evening air; a trio of crows flapped heavily towards the mountain; and the stonechats chatted among the stones. The sweet smell of turf smoke filled the doctor's nostrils, plumes of it rising straight up in the damp stillness from the odd small cabin dotted around the bogland. Decaying piles of turf lay by the side of the bog road, evidence of the many days stretching out into months without enough dry weather to even think about bringing it home. Tonight, perhaps, he would re-write one last time that crucial first chapter of *The History*. As he walked, he rehearsed the phrasing in his mind, turning the words over and trying them out this way and that.

When Dr. O'Toole returned home from his walk he found his daughter Niamh knitting by the little turf fire. That girl was forever working the needles, he thought; ah, how she reminded him of her departed mother - her pale skin, green eyes and dark hair, all classic features of Inishower ancestry; her hunched, tense posture and furrowed brow; her ceaseless knitting; and most of all her way of hitting you around the head with a wet mackerel when you've done wrong. The fondness that both women had for that particular denizen of the sea was surely unnatural; neither would be seen for very long without one of the shiny creatures in her hand. The doctor was intimately familiar with the swishing sound that preceded the jarring, jolting slap across the side of the skull on the occasion of his many transgressions.

Automatically he eyed Niamh to check out the indicator of her mood - the status of the island women's furrowed brow that was known as the Knitter's Cleft of Inishower. The doctor knew that single deep vertical line very well; for nigh on fifty years it had been his barometer of emotional weather in the home, first in Molly and the mother-in-law, then in Niamh. It was the early warning system that had saved him from the mackerel clout on more than one occasion. Now it was on a reading of about six - a little on the high side, but nothing to worry about.

"That's a fine evening," said the doctor.

"It is," said Niamh.

"An evening Molly would have loved."

"Indeed." Niamh's brow softened and the cleft went down a couple of points more. It usually did when she thought of her mother. The doctor's mind too turned to his wife. He could see her now as if she had departed only the day before - the fair skin, the sea-green eyes and the black hair gone to silver.

They were both silent. The doctor knew his daughter wasn't happy; maybe this was the moment to broach the subject - perhaps offer her a bit of fatherly support; for he thought he knew what the problem was. A moment like this with the cleft on such a low reading didn't happen every day. He wondered how to start.

But now the scene of Molly's demise came into the doctor's mind, as clear as yesterday; he still blamed himself; perhaps he could have prevented it somehow. But how was he to know that she would go and throw herself under an unloading boatload of her favourite seafood? Yet he knew in his heart that it was his own indiscretions that had driven her to it. Gone to grey with worry, was the truth about her hair. He blamed himself - and he knew that Niamh blamed him too. Now the moment had passed, and the cleft had deepened once more.

"I'd best be getting on with *The History*," said the doctor quickly, and headed straight for his study.

A Brief History of Inishower

by Dr. Ulick O'Toole

The history of Inishower is an endless story of invasions, disillusionment, literary conundrums, and excessive moisture. The moisture has always been the most important thing.

Inishower is a small island in the Atlantic ocean, flung far from the nearest coast of Ireland. Its seaward cliffs are perpetually assaulted by battering swells, while the landward shores are blessed with sheltered inlets and placid strands. The island's most striking physical feature is the towering, twin-peaked Sleabh Lasc Eireaball or Fishtail Mountain at the seaward end, which has exerted a ubiquitous influence on the local topography, weather systems, history and culture. Its broad mass directly faces the wet westerly airstream that blows in steadily over thousands of miles of open sea;

its stubborn obstructiveness causes the air to rise abruptly and drop wetness over the island even in the driest of times. Thus is created Inishower's unique microclimatic system - a cloud that covers the island at all times in varying degrees of density, with never a moment when it isn't raining in one way or another. Innumerable ships have come to grief on the jagged surfbound reefs of the Devil's Quills at the foot of the mountain, obscured by the legendary mists that can descend at any time of day or night.

Fishtail Mountain, in all its shrouded mystery, has always been the prime focus of local lore and superstition. It is held sacred and greatly feared, and to this day few locals will set foot upon its upper reaches. Filled with grim foreboding on even a relatively bright day, it looms over life on the island, a subtle yet ever-present influence on daily affairs.

The island's soggy, rain-soaked atmosphere stands alongside Inishower's other outstanding characteristic - an extraordinary heritage of literary development. Historians have come up with many complex theories to explain this phenomenon, but in the opinion of this author the connection is straightforward: writers here simply stay at home all day, every day, and get on with the job of writing, because of the weather. There isn't anything else for them to do.

U.o'T.

4 Much Ado about Nothing Much

The light that evening had all but faded, yet Niamh was still knitting when Malachy Moodie came in the back door with dragging feet. Niamh smiled and put down her knitting to greet him, but Malachy only threw a bag of wet mackerel in her lap. His fair hair was unkempt and his face had more than a day's stubble on it. His strong build, swarthy skin and smouldering brown eyes too set him apart from the rest of the islanders. His woollen boatman's jumper and boots were in disrepair and his trousers covered in boat oil.

Malachy was clearly not in good mood, even though the summer was the best time for him. Malachy was Inishower's sole boatman. Everything brought to the island was brought by him. When the festival started he would be raking it in, ferrying visitors over from the mainland in his boat as well as carrying on with his regular fishing. In summertime Malachy was merely sulky; at other seasons he was worse. Malachy, sadly, was an outsider; one of those unfortunate individuals who couldn't take the perpetual rain. It was hardly his fault that he'd been dumped on the island as an infant and brought up by strangers, now long passed on. Inishower really was no place for him, yet he couldn't leave either - he wanted Niamh too much – but you'd hardly know it from the way he got on.

"What's for dinner?" Malachy pouted as he sat down in the corner.

"Mackerel," Niamh replied, abandoning attempts at warmth. She well knew that their relationship wasn't working. She opened the bag and moved to the kitchen table to prepare the fish; just out of the sea, their silver sides and vivid zigzag markings glistened with iridescence in the twilight. She had made her play for Malachy seven years before. But now the whole thing between them was a bit like one of those mackerel that had gone bad, it now seemed to her. Once it had been young and fresh, bright and shiny and moist; but now it had become dull and dry and would leave a terrible taste in your mouth. She tore off the fish heads and ripped out their insides with strong fingers, as she'd done a thousand times before.

"Oh Malachy!" she cried suddenly, looking up from the pile of guts in front of her. "What is happening to us? Where have all our shiny bits and moistness gone?"

"What in the name of Jaysus are you talkin' about, woman?" he said, then paused. "- And have you done knitting that new pullover for me yet?"

"I haven't. It'll be finished soon," she replied, avoiding his eyes as she said it.

Niamh knew the partnership was hopeless; yet she carried on pretending that it was still working. The problem was that no one on the island but Malachy knew how to catch mackerel; the others were all writers; and she couldn't live without mackerel. A girl had to consider such things. And so they staggered on together with their dysfunctional liaison. She was having trouble getting motivated about the new jumper, too. She wasn't enjoying making it, and hadn't made any progress with it for weeks, if the truth be told. That was another crucial aspect of their partnership: incompatibility in the woollens department, central to the life of any knitter on Inishower. Still, maybe those things could change, she kept telling herself; maybe a miracle would happen. But then there was the sexual thing, most crucial of all; that had never been right, if she was honest with herself. The man simply did not have the uniquely formed reproductive apparatus of the natural-born Inishovian male. Malachy did not possess the *Inishower Prong*, and nothing could ever be done about that.

5 A La Research du Temps Perdu

Writing was the business of the Inishovians - the only thing they could do well, apart from the knitting of course. It was the cottage industry and the export commodity - the only way they knew how to make any money. After all those millennia of authorial activity, the writing gene was firmly embedded in the islanders' DNA. Those who had no interest in it generally emigrated, or quickly died off owing to the rain-sodden depression that set in if you had no inner richness of imagination to get you through. Yet for those of an extreme literary bent, Inishower could be an ideal environment; and if you didn't mind the rain either, it was something of a paradise.

Inishower Literary Festival was the high point - indeed the only point - of the Inishovian year, and now it was the mainstay of the island economy as well. Each year in mid-August visitors flocked in from far and wide for three glorious weeks of solid readings, workshops and alcohol-fuelled literary activity. But as the Inishovian saying goes, every silver lining has a cloud around it; and even now Dr. O'Toole could see clouds gathering on the metaphoric horizon. Inishower was now on the literary map; every year more people were turning up for it. Obscure American academics had been coming over for years - their purchases of every original manuscript, letter or scribbled-on envelope that they could get their hands on was a considerable source of finance. But now, as well as those who were welcome, there was an increasingly unsavoury element of literary ne'er-do-wells - the gutterati, as the doctor called them - a verbally challenged bunch of posers, chancers and hangers-on. And the worst of the lot were those would-be authors who never did any writing - people who vaguely hoped that just being on the island would somehow turn them into paragons of productivity. 'I'm sure I have a book inside me,' these people would remark to Mickey Squigley, proprietor of Squigley's Handy Bar and Rainwear Store in the village. Mickey, no mean writer himself, would mutter that inside of them was maybe where such a book might best remain.

Nevertheless, the festival's ever-increasing prestige brought distinct advantages to the doctor, not least when it came to claiming hedonistic favours in exchange for including candidates in the programme. And that was an important asset to him - very important.

So at last it was the start of the literary season on Inishower. Visitors would fight for accommodation in one or other of the island's only two hotels, or have to rent a bed in a cramped cabin half-way up the mountain. Now there would be non-stop readings and signings, lectures and workshops, dinner parties and soirées and matinées, sessions and shenanigans, hooleys and ceilidhs and flings. At the end of three weeks the visitors would depart - save for the inevitable two or three that would stay on, lured by infatuation for a local resident or by the favourable tax status for writers, or maybe just trapped by the strangely charged inertia of the place.

Today the first influx of festival-goers from the outside world would arrive. Now Dr O'Toole stood on the jetty - with his hands in his pockets just in case hedonistic opportunities arose - and watched Malachy's packed boat approach the tiny harbour where the rocks of Inishower Island plunged into the Atlantic waters. It was another fairly fine day, with only a hint of spumy sleet. In the gentlest of swells the sea kelp could be seen gently moving in the clear depths - provided you put your face right on top of the water.

Malachy glumly steered the boat in to the quay and began to push the occupants ashore. It was not every day that he could take the boat across on the long trip to the mainland; and some of the visitors had spent a week on the other side waiting for a dry enough day for the boat not to fill up with rain on the way over. Another couple of boatloads were still waiting over there, and it looked like a storm might be brewing. Malachy hated the festival – he'd have to make hundreds of trips to and fro to get everyone over. As the island's only boatman he could charge them what he liked, but he still used it to fuel a resentment that deepened and widened and festered year upon year.

It was always a similar mix of people that came, the doctor observed to himself - more or less the same medley of literary sorts, even though the overall numbers rose steadily each year - as if some sort of adaptable algebra was at work to keep a mysterious balance between the various bookish influences and genres.

He quantified and categorised, ticking them off as they managed to get ashore. The angry-looking ones that pushed their way off the boat first were of course the young Turks. They were always fiercely aware of their youth and their genius, full of assuredness that the literary future was theirs. Yet each year a brand-new group of them would arrive, just as angry and full of genius and assuredness; but somewhere back home on the mainland would be last year's young Turks, passed over by the trendmongers of literary fashion - bewildered and dismayed and wondering what had happened to the literary future that had so assuredly been theirs. Yet the doctor still relished the belligerent, discordant note that they introduced to the festival during their brief trajectories of stardom.

Closely following these would be the writers of the so-called chemical generation with their associated groupies, hangers-on, babes and wannabes. These were attracted in part by the literary ambience on the island, but mainly by the progressive policing policy; that is to say, the nearest Garda being on the other side of the water and not at all keen to visit. So these adventurers looked forward to three solid weeks of doing drugs, giving readings about doing drugs, and corrupting the native islanders into doing drugs.

Then there were the many enthusiasts who had made the great pilgrimage via the mainland, from America. Most of these maintained that they had whiskeybottlefuls of Irish literary blood coursing through their veins; they dreamed of tracing long-lost ancestry right back to the island itself, yearning to unblock some vast unstoppable flow of the volcanic lava of writerly creativity that they reckoned must lie dormant below the calm surface of their personal genetic pool. Their uniform goal invariably seemed to be the execution of fat epic books that would span myriad generations across numerous continents and encapsulate the whole philosophy of humankind. They'd go straight to McDadgh's.

There were many familiar faces too, individuals who came year after year. Most flamboyant of the regulars were the English eccentrics, Lancelot and Bryony de Boyle and their coterie, who enjoyed the place so much they had given up summering in Sussex for the joys of Inishower's little season. Now they returned each year to swap sexual partners and devise ingenious liaisons amongst themselves, while decorating their usual cottage with outrageous and explicit scenes of carnal libidity; when their own permutations and possibilities were exhausted, they would endeavour to entice the locals into their strange trisexual ways. But what was the harm in that, the doctor reasoned; they brought good trade to the island - and a further degree of welcome notoriety, it could be argued.

And of course there was a motley crew of other odds and ends: secretive literary agents and talent scouts, slim authors of slim volumes of poetry, new Asian writers of taboo-busting raga-sagas, surrealists and situationists, post-modernists and deconstructionists; plus assorted journalists, party-goers, low-life and hoipolloi who only pretended to be interested in literature - the *gutterati*. How familiar he was with the range of stereotyped emotion displayed by them all, from genuine and innocent excitedness to carefully cultivated gloom or jaded petulance.

The doctor dismissed any trace of misgiving that he might have had, and watched as the last of the passengers stepped ashore. His spirits rose as he observed a healthy number of fresh-faced, fresh-bodied female arrivals; he felt the evident relish take physical form in his trousers, for his hands were already in his pockets. Surely it was going to be the best Inishower Literary Festival yet. The launch wasn't for some days, but the doctor's favourite component - his own summer school - would begin the next day. And meanwhile he would do his best to garner the most succulent of the crop of new arrivals into his scholastic lap.

6 Le Grand Moan

Down at the library next day, Dr. O'Toole surveyed the gathering of students for his first masterclass. His efforts of the previous evening had ensured that they were suitably numerous, satisfyingly enthusiastic and exclusively female. That was how he liked it; especially when his topic for the course was *Writing Hot Sex*.

The doctor had just given them their first assignment - five hundred words on *Setting the Scene for Seduction* - and they were all working away at it. He could already distinguish which candidates were most likely to turn in the kind of work that interested him. Deirdre O'Dowdy from Belfast, for instance, was still staring at a blank page with a pained, stuck look that betrayed her strict convent upbringing on the Falls Road: hopeless. Modesty Thinkwell, over from England, was writing a lot but going back to cross it all out; that wouldn't be much good either. Then there was Sally-Anne Peachley, the tanned southern belle from Tallahassee - she was easily the most promising. In just ten minutes she had written fifteen or sixteen pages, in a fluid hand-written script. Oblivious to the world, she worked with intense concentration, the tip of her tongue frequently moistening her full, red pouting lips. She tossed the bubbly blonde locks of her transatlantically big hair this way and that without a trace of self-consciousness. Her breath grew audibly heavier; her neat bottom squirmed on her chair, and he could hear her make little whimpering sounds. This was clearly an individual who had no trouble with abandon. Pheromones fairly flew from her, bearing the promise of steamy coursework to come. By the look of things she had gone well past *Setting the Scene* and got heavily into the next day's assignment, *On The Job*. The doctor liked a woman who was unable to defer gratification. He had the distinct impression that he was going to be very pleased with her work.

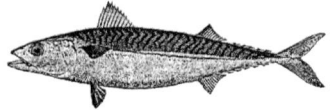

7 Angela's Orifices

Dr O'Toole ran his literary surgery every Wednesday morning, and it proved especially popular during the festival for it was widely known that he also used these sessions as opportunities to 'audition' would-be literary contributors to festival events. The doctor sat at his large oak desk that was covered with handwritten papers. The wood-panelled walls surrounding him were lined with heavily laden bookshelves more worthy of a library.

The storm of the last few days had almost blown itself out as Angela Blossom entered. She looked to be in her mid-forties, smartly dressed with the appearance of someone who lived life to the full, the doctor thought. She had laughed a lot and cried a lot; the crow's feet round her eyes had grown into something more like raven's. But that was fine. He appreciated a woman who had experience, especially if she could let herself go.

"Angela," said the doctor, with excessive bedside in his manner. "Tell me, what seems to be the problem?"

"It's my sex scenes. I don't know...they just seem to be lacking something. My characters aren't getting turned on at all easily."

"A common problem," said the doctor, with deliberate sympathy. "It's experienced by almost all women of your...position." That was close; he had almost said 'age'. "But it can be cured. I'll need to do an examination, obviously. Just go behind that screen and slip off your things."

"Is that really necessary?"

"You do want to get better, don't you?"

"Well, yes..."

"Better enough for me to consider featuring your work in the festival?"

"Ah yes, I see what you mean. Well, of course I'm happy to try anything that will improve my prospects."

The things were duly slipped off. It was working.

"Now I'm going to go through a number of procedures, and I want you to describe them as I do so - as a writer would, you see. As if you were another person watching us, and writing about it. In the third person. I find it can be very..." - he almost said 'arousing' - "...effective. You know, things like 'He cupped her ample breast in his hand; she could no longer resist the tide of passion that rose within her...' that sort of thing. I think you'll find it very um... helpful."

At this point something changed perceptibly in the geometry of the anterior aureole of her left nipple. That was good. He also noticed a distinct increase in his own salivation. It looked like this really was going to work. In his trousers, a trout rose to a fly. She noticed, and smiled.

"Do you have a license for that?" asked Angela.

"I do indeed. A poetic license."

Angela laughed. It was looking good. The raven's feet deepened into stork's. Laughing generously at his jokes: that was attractive in a woman. He savoured the moment. He didn't hear the door open, but he did detect the familiar swish and he certainly felt the wet, stinging slap as a heavy fish nearly burst his right eardrum. It was Niamh, mackerel in hand.

"Not again, father!" She grabbed Angela's things from behind the screen and threw them at her. "End of consultation!" she spat, and shoved the other woman roughly out of the room. "Is it any wonder my mother died so young?" she yelled at the doctor as she left.

"Shite," said the doctor to himself as tears stung his eyes, "I nearly made it that time."

8 The Hoarse Whisperer

Finbar McFogarty - Inishower grocer, writer of pulp non-fiction and general nosy parker, pushed his head round the surgery door. Dr. O'Toole was reading student work and breathing heavily, with a glazed, slightly delirious look in his eye.

"Have you heard the news, doctor? There's a man washed up on the eastern beach with bits of a boat. You'd best come up and see what you can do!"

At that particular moment, a man washed up on the beach was the last thing on the doctor's mind, for he was working his way through a pile of Sally-Anne Peachley's latest offerings.

"Can you not bring him down here yourself?" he asked Finbar.

"We tried picking him up, but he's making a fierce crackling noise. I'd say every bone in his body is broken from the sound of it."

"Is he conscious or unconscious?"

"Somewhere in between, I'd say. He's making a very dry raspy kind of a noise in his throat. He doesn't sound good at all."

The doctor reluctantly dragged his attention from the papers, put them in a folder, stowed it in the bottom drawer and locked it, safely away from prying filial eyes. "I'd better come down."

Down at the eastern beach, a small crowd of onlookers stood in the drizzle, gathering round the body lying crumpled on the sand. It was a tallish, lean-looking man who might have been in his early fifties, dressed in a navy blue seagoing sweater and oily black trousers with no footwear in sight. He had white crinkly hair and a beard, with dense, bushy eyebrows and an aquiline nose. His eyes were closed. His face looked white and powdery, and his feet, ankles and hands were the same. Nearby was a sizeable leather covered box that had taken a fair bashing in the sea, but was still intact.

The man was breathing sporadically; as he did so, a faint creaking sound came from his chest. Dry scraping noises escaped from his mouth. The doctor picked up one limp hand to feel for a pulse, and even from this small movement heard the crackling noise for himself; yet the man did not wince in the slightest. It was strange indeed. O'Toole thought for some moments. Then he pulled back the sleeve and observed that the white powdery effect was there too; indeed, it seemed to be on every part of the man's skin. He touched the powder, and dabbed it on his tongue.

"Throw a bucket of water over him," he said to Finbar.

The men brought a bucket from a nearby house, and went to the sea to fill it.

"Not sea water," said the doctor impatiently "- fresh water."

The water was duly replaced, and the man doused with it.

"Fetch another one."

"To throw over him?" asked Finbar.

"No. For him to drink."

When this was brought, the man's head was raised with further crackling, and he was given water. When a couple of glasses were got into him, he seemed the better for it. He lifted his head as if to speak. The doctor placed his ear near the man's mouth. The sound was clearer this time.

"Inishower," he croaked. "Take me to Inishower."

"You're in it already," the doctor said. "This is Inishower."

"Ah...!" the man gasped, and rested his head back down again.

"Bring him up to the surgery," the doctor said to the men standing around.

"But what about all the broken bones?" asked Finbar.

"Never mind that. Throw a couple more buckets of water over him and bring him on up."

They drenched him again and then picked him up.

"Bejaysus, what's inside this man? He weighs a ton!"

"I think he's saying something else," said Finbar. The doctor listened closely.

"The box," the man rasped, "bring my box!"

"Bring the box as well," the doctor ordered.

Back at the surgery, the doctor took down his 1887 edition of *Purdey's Ailments of the Human Organism* and scrutinised it closely. The new arrival was lying flat out on the day bed, his eyes closed. The white cakey substance was substantially less visible on his skin, which now had a bit of colour. He looked a lot better. Though clearly still weak, he was breathing almost creaklessly.

The doctor smiled as he found the entry he was looking for. Indeed, he was so absorbed by what he read that he quite forgot Sally-Anne's manuscript still in his bottom drawer:

Sclerosis Saliensis

An extremely rare condition in which the patient's entire system becomes saturated with salt. This occurs as a result of de Beauvoir's Syndrome, a dietary phenomenon wherein the candidate is compulsively obsessed with the ingestion of sodium chloride. Only patients who are possessed of an unusually robust cardiac constitution are able to survive perpetual salt poisoning, including terminally high blood pressure and risk of heart attack, which de Beauvoir's Syndrome produces. Associated characteristics of the condition include continuous exudation of salt through the skin, crystalline deposits in the joints, and psychological fixation upon things to do with salt, the sea and seafish.

Professor Antoine de Beauvoir of Bruges University, whose life's work was the study of the disease, suffered from it himself; if it were not for his studies, this most intriguing condition would no doubt remain undiagnosed today. It is interesting to note that after death, the bodies of sufferers of de Beauvoir's Syndrome have been found to resist decomposition almost indefinitely; de Beauvoir opined that Sclerosis Saliensis may have been endemic among the pharoic elite in ancient Egypt. The professor himself, however, was destined never to enjoy the posthumous benefits of such natural mummification. He died tragically during one of his experiments upon himself, endeavouring to find a permanent cure for the illness by applying an electrical current. Owing to the inordinately high level of electrolytes in salt, sufferers of Sclerosis Saliensis are extremely efficient conductors, and M. de Beauvoir was no exception. His ashes are now preserved in the Museum of Necropsy in Hyderabad.

The only known cure for Sclerosis Saliensis involves a more or less continuous regime of immersion in fresh water.

9 Captain Flaherty's Organ

Dr. O'Toole awoke the following morning to music drifting up from downstairs. The tune was a slow air of mournful mood; the sound was not unlike that of a concertina, but somehow more religious in tone, bringing to mind the soporific sermons he used to hear as a child very long ago in the little island chapel. The music seemed familiar, though he knew for certain that he had not heard anything quite like it before. It touched the spirit, he noted, more than the physical ear. And it had a discernible effect on the senses - soothing, calming and reassuring, he would say. It was intriguing.

The doctor got up from his bed and stepped quietly down the stairs, approaching the source of the sound in his surgery. The door was open just a fraction. He could see the newcomer now, on the daybed. The man was sitting up quite straight, with his own dry clothes on him again. His movements were still somewhat stiff and he crackled a bit but he looked a lot younger now, and his eyes were a bright grey. He was absorbed in the music he was making, a million miles away by the look of it. The open box sat near him on the floor, and strapped to the inside of the lid was a brass telescope. The doctor glimpsed parts of the instrument as he played. It had a squeezebox like an accordion, with a keyboard at one side and buttons at the other, but there was also a set of upright pipes from which the sound appeared to come. These were made of some sort of dull ivory, slightly spirallic in form, and carved with tiny images of fishes and animals.

The doctor entered the room. The music stopped. The man smiled at him, and a sea of wrinkles sprang into action in his face.

"You're looking more like yourself this morning," said the doctor, extending his hand. "Dr. Ulick O'Toole at your service."

The handshake crackled. "Captain Flaherty. I am indeed more like myself." His accent was hard to place, a mixture of things such as you'd find on the beach after a storm. There was Irish in there certainly, but bits of other stuff floating around as well - hints of America and maybe something further afield too. "And I'm indebted to you, I believe."

"Ah, not at all."

"So this is Inishower. I've heard a lot about it," Captain Flaherty went on. "...But how's my boat?"

"I'm sorry to say the boat's in bits - done for entirely. You got snagged on the Devil's Quills. You were lucky that you drifted round to the eastern shore with the wreckage."

"There was a mist. I never saw one come down as sudden as that, right in the middle of a storm too. I couldn't see my own hand."

"That mist is always there at the mountainy end of the island; you would need to have to come in at the other side. You're not the first to go wrong there, and you won't be the last...But are you here for the festival?"

"Festival? Ah no. I heard about Inishower and thought I'd give it a try. I was just curious really."

The doctor was curious too. "Well, you can stay here for a day or two if you want," he said. "It's going to take you a while to recover. Are you hungry at all?"

"I am indeed."

"What do you fancy?"

"I could murder a couple of mackerel."

"I think we can cater for such a crime as that. But what's that instrument? I never saw one of those before."

"I don't believe there's a name for it. I got it from my father. There was only maybe half a dozen of them ever made, by a Newfoundland man called Jebediah Cruste, around 1760, my grandfather said. Mr. Cruste hunted for furs in the far north, and invented a variety of musical instruments when the weather was bad. He got the pipes from the Inuits - they're made from the tusks of Narwhals, very light but tough. The Inuit hunters believed that the sound attracts whales and seals and such creatures. Cruste had the idea of using them to make instruments like this." He blew a few more bars and listened intently, sensing the notes for himself, as if to check that they still worked. "This one came into my great-grandfather's possession in 1801, when he worked on a whaler up and down the coast of North America, and it stayed in my family. My father became Pastor of the Church of the Wretched Seamen in Nova Scotia." He played a couple more chords in a plaintive key. "I remember him accompanying hymns in the wee tin chapel. There was never any shortage of congregation when he played."

Now he launched into a livelier tune; a sea shanty by the sound of it, with decoration and wild notes here and there. The doctor listened intently; he could hear the winds of the wide ocean in it, and the cries of gulls, and maybe there was an albatross soaring high in the open sky. It was the sort of sound that takes you on a journey, in a drifting kind of consciousness after which you couldn't quite say where you'd been. Then the music stopped.

"What about those mackerel?" said the captain after a while.

The doctor came back from far away. "We'll see what can be done," he said, getting up to find Niamh. There was something very interesting about all this.

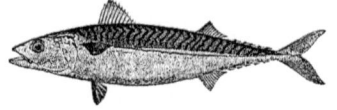

10 A Walk on the Mild Side

"Breakfast's ready!" called Niamh O'Toole with some severity. "Are yis coming in for it?"

The doctor dutifully sidled in from the surgery followed by the captain. He quickly checked the cleft on Niamh's brow; it was on about seven.

Niamh eyed the captain with little friendliness. That was a bad sweater he had on, she thought. It was one of the worst sweaters she had seen in a long time. What was in the mind of the person who had knitted it? What kind of a woman would do a thing like that? There wasn't an ounce of craftsmanship in it. The knit was as loose as a dead donkey's droppings. It wasn't going to keep the weather out for a minute. She could tell it had been made by a *graighaeoil*[1] - maybe not even an Irish *graighaeoil*. And what kind of a man would wear such a knitted garment? She wasn't a bit pleased when her father took in people like this. The sooner he was on his way, the better.

"This is Captain Flaherty," said the doctor. "Captain Flaherty, my daughter Niamh."

"I know," said Niamh.

"Delighted to make your acquaintance," said the captain. The doctor noticed that his eye had a bit of a sparkle in it today. The island climate was suiting him rather well.

They sat down at the big wooden kitchen table that was worn down in the middle with the gutting of fish. Niamh put down plates in front of them and splattered out a fat cooked mackerel for each of them.

"That's all there is in the house," she said.

---

[1] abusive term for a mainlander

"That'll be grand," said the captain, tucking in. "Thanks very much."

Niamh watched out of the corner of her eye as he deftly peeled off the skin from the midline upwards and downwards, and discarded the flesh next the abdomen which can get a bitter taste from the innards if the fish is more than an hour out of the sea. Then he delicately lifted a portion of flesh above the lateral line away from the bone; that was the sweetest portion. He seemed to know his way round the fish, anyway. Then he spoiled it.

"Have you a bit more salt?"

Niamh threw the heavy stone salt grinder in his direction. The captain caught it deftly, as if anticipating that mode of delivery.

"Niamh, where are your manners?" asked the doctor.

"I wasn't very well brought up."

What's got into that girl? the doctor wondered.

The Captain dosed his fish heavily with salt and continued eating. He was soon finished.

"Delicious," he said. "Have you another couple of those?"

"There's more of them in the sea, I've heard," Niamh replied. "But you'll have to wait till Malachy goes out again."

"Is that so?" said the captain thoughtfully.

After dinner Dr. O'Toole was inclined to invite the captain to join him on his evening perambulatory meditation out behind the house and over the bog road. This did not go unnoticed by Niamh; it was an unheard-of departure from his long-standing pattern of solitariness in brooding on the island and its ways. But whatever she thought, it was the doctor's inclination to offer the invitation and it was the captain's inclination to accept.

As the two men walked out of the back of the house they felt the fine soft evening drizzle and still air, which were Dr. O'Toole's favourite weather for contemplative review. The doctor paused before the back gate, while the captain maintained a respectful silence. The two of them looked out over the bog meadows that stretched gently towards the base of the mountain, taking in the tangible peacefulness of the setting. From a far-off field they heard the plaintive cry of the curlew, leaving a silence in its wake that seemed deeper still.

Presently the doctor opened the gate and strode out on the narrow bog road. The captain walked by his side, stiffly at first but soon loosening up; and this may have been partly what Dr. O'Toole had in mind. The white heads of the bog cotton standing in the water seemed to grow luminous as the light began to fade. The doctor knew every bog plant well. The Mistberries shone on their small bushes, almost ripe now. Blossoms of deceptively attractive Dank Maiden's Pouch tinged the air with a faintly fishy aroma. The insectivorous Sogwort, with its sticky dew-edged leaves, glistened at the water's edges, waiting in vain to trap any insects that ventured out in the drizzle. Only the most sturdy of the early evening moths flitted over the flowers, enjoying the absence of a downpour.

Eventually the doctor began to speak. He spoke of the unique range of water plants that inhabited the damp landscape: the Bog Myrtle and Bog Bean; the gently glowing Water Hyacinth, and the sadness of the Weeping Goosegrass; the Wet Lettuce, Sogwort and Sodden Sorrel. The ancient peoples of this island, he told the captain, believed that they could immunise themselves against the inroads of moisture by ingesting minute quantities of the moisture-saturated plants; and the doctor maintained that this was the earliest occurrence of homeopathy in any culture.

All across the bogland, the layers of wet turf had been sliced away, leaving the clean-cut banks like moist fruit cake. At the foot of each vertical face was a narrow pool of dark water. To these pools, the doctor said, the seers used to come in ancient times - to read the future of the island, to discover what conquering forces would come next, and to see if there was ever going to be a change in the weather. These people were known as the 'scrying hags', and it was certainly true that the task always fell to the least beauteous women of the island. They would peer into the dark waters and discern images of ships crossing the sea, bringing weapons and unfamiliar instruments of learning. And the only change in the weather that they would ever see would be one for the worse. So it wasn't a great job, or indeed a popular one.

    The captain asked penetrating questions. The doctor went on to expound on the history of the island, on the successive waves of settlers and conquerors and their respective strands of literary tradition. He explained the details of their culture and the remnants that had survived in island life. He told of the language and the lore, and gave the names of things and their meanings. He spoke at length from his considerable store of knowledge about the rain. And the captain appeared to take it all in.

    Farther down the road, a heron rose from a stretch of open water at the foot of a turf bank, a speckled brown trout wriggling in its beak, and made off with slow and heavy flaps. In the distance they could just discern the brooding presence of Fishtail Mountain standing over the scene, with its perpetual mantle of dense cloud above the mists. The captain seemed to be at ease with it all - the land, the lore and the language that the doctor opened up to him. He seemed at ease, too, in the soft misty rain, moving more easily, invaded by the fluidity of the environment. In the thickening twilight air the doctor sensed his immersion in all of this, and was quietly pleased.

The following evening after dinner they walked together once more. This time the rain was heavier, yet the captain still seemed to relish it. The doctor intimated his life work, the historical archiving of the island lore. When they got home, he took the captain to the room where he stored the archives in their many drafts and redrafts. It would once have been a walk-in pantry, quite a large windowless room on the northern side of the house with shelves round all its walls, each stacked neatly with bundles of manuscript tied up with stout lengths of rough red-dyed sheepswool. On each shelf and below each pile of papers was tiny lettering with archival headings - The Neolithic Era; The Celtic Twilight; The Nordic Influx, and so on, into their hundreds. Then there was a bundle of documentation for each year of the festival, plus miscellaneous subject topics; by far the largest of which was Precipitative Influences. Dr Ulick O'Toole was clearly a man who was fond of establishing the order of things. The captain observed all this and was not unimpressed.

The evening after that, on their third damp outing, the captain strode out smoothly, and the doctor turned his attention to finding out more about his companion. But the man did not seem to enjoy talking about himself. All the doctor got was an impression that he was looking for something but was not sure what it was; and that meanwhile he'd spent a fair bit of time seeking escape from the enduring discomfort of his creaking body and restless soul. The two of them spent the rest of that walk discussing salt, a subject brought up by the doctor. When they got home and the captain had retired, the doctor sat up late, inspired to re-work yet again his discourses on some of the key periods of Inishower's damp past.

The Early Days

The very first wave of settlers on Inishower are thought to have come in Neolithic times, hard on the heels of the receding ice sheets - those great stretches of frozen water that saturated everything as they melted. And the later generations of these stone-age people became the first European progenitors of the written word, in the form of simple scratches cut into the edges of large monoliths of rock. This is how it came about. Because of the constantly inclement weather, folks were forever shut up together in their caves, so that they would constantly get on one another's nerves and stop speaking to one other. The beginnings of written communication thus evolved to solve this problem, and came to be known as Ugham. These hieroglyphics are generally thought to have had a disgruntlement-expressing function; the most frequently recurring theme being distaste for their totally raw diet, together with pleas to their deities for the speedy invention of cooking. A historical point worth mentioning here is that the Paleolithic era on Inishower skipped out the entirety of the Bronze and Iron Ages, because in these most watery of post-glacial times nobody could ever get a fire going to do any metal-working.

While their pioneering contemporaries elsewhere worshipped the deities of the sun, moon and stars, the so-called Ughees honoured only the forces that most controlled their lives: the rain gods, the deities of Fishtail Mountain, and the spirits of the spoken and written word. For Ughees didn't see enough of the sun, moon or stars to believe in them properly; but as with most early shamanic cultures, animal totems were powerful sources of inspiration and of protective energies. Naturally, water-related creatures with qualities that the Ughees considered most vital were key candidates. The heron, for instance, could bestow the much-prized ability to stand around for a long time doing nothing, and the newt embodied the spirit of drinking and inebriation. But most sacred of all was the beaver, a powerful fertility symbol because of its association with the female procreative genitalia.

U.o'T.

11 August is a Fishy Month

The doctor woke late next morning in a state of mounting excitement; the following day would be the official opening of the festival. Entering the kitchen he found his daughter sitting at the table, looking mightily displeased. The cleft was on about eight.

"What's for breakfast?" he asked in an attempt at cheeriness.

"Nothing," said Niamh. "There's no mackerel."

"No mackerel? Where's Malachy then?"

"He's disappeared. No one's seen him since the day before yesterday. His boat's in the harbour, though. Nobody in the village has any mackerel."

From the daybed in the surgery, Captain Flaherty listened with interest. Then he quickly got up, dressed, picked up the musical instrument in its case, and quietly made his way through the hallway, out the front door and down to the harbour.

At about noon the doctor thought he'd walk into the village and make sure that final arrangements were in place for the festival opening at Mickey Squigley's the next day. There were things to do, people to see, and insecure literary personages needing careful reassurance that their role was crucial to the success of the venture.

As the doctor walked towards Squigley's pub at the harbour - the village's main hub of communication and number one venue for any kind of public event - he noticed quite a gathering of people on the pier, all watching a boat that was approaching from round the headland. He walked over to take a look. It looked like Malachy was coming in, and the boat was low in the water. Was he bringing more precious literary cargo of punters and personages?

But as the boat drew near to the quay, the doctor could see that it was weighed down not with people but with fish - mackerel, and a lot of them. And it was not being steered by Malachy but by Captain Flaherty. The crowd was fairly buzzing and the boat was docking by the time the doctor reached the near end of the quay. What were they so excited about? Was it that the captain had been fishing in Malachy's boat? Then the doctor realised that the only things in the boat were the captain, the mackerel and his organ case. There was no sign of lines, nets or any other instruments of fishing; Malachy must have taken them away with him. Everybody was wondering about this too; that's what the buzz was all about. But if anybody was asking the captain how he had managed this trick he wasn't saying, or the answer would have been round the crowd in a flash.

The captain greeted the doctor and handed him a dozen or so of the fattest fish, still vivid with their vivid black zig-zag bars on blue and green and their bright silver sides. "I expect Niamh could use a couple of these," he said.

"I expect she could. How did you manage that?"

"Ah, they must have been jumping into the boat of their own accord," replied the captain with a grin. "I suppose it's just my lucky day." And he began to hand out free fish to all and sundry - a thing that Malachy hadn't done in fifteen years, it was widely noted. If a person had ever wanted to become popular on Inishower, it wouldn't have been a bad way to start.

12 Catch 23½

Mickey Squigley's Handy Hotel Bar and Rainwear Store was fairly buzzing for the official opening of Inishower Literary Festival. Mickey presided behind the bar, lord of all he surveyed.

Mickey himself was probably the island's leading authority on rainfall and the prevention of its ingress to the human skin, and was often consulted by Dr. O'Toole on matters of finer precipitative detail in the interests of accuracy in *The History*. Indeed, the man was an all-round specialist in matters concerning fluids, as would befit the island's leading publican; he sometimes referred to himself as a 'hydraulic entrepreneur'. Mickey had a great nose for the weather altogether; it was said that he could identify ninety-seven different kinds of precipitation and predict which of these would fall on any day next week. Naturally he also pulled the best and slowest pint of bog-stout on the island. Visible evidence of the care and commitment he put into this could be seen in the number of pint glasses lined up on the top of the bar at any time, in various stages of settling and topping up. At busy times these could number a hundred, as they did today.

Squigley's was more like a department store with hospitality than a regular pub. The main bar, the traditional venue for most of the festival events, displayed rainwear of every conceivable kind. It was lined with rails of overcoats, anoraks and kagouls, lightweight pac-a-macs, capes and gabardines, heavy-duty trenchcoats and slickers, robust oilskins and tarpcoats with triple seams and inviolable detailing. There were sou'westers, nor'easters and gear that repelled wind and rain from every other major point of the compass. There was another whole section full of boots, galoshes, wellingtons and the thigh-length overshoes that were popular on Inishower in the winter, since nothing less would serve any useful purpose here. In the hat department there was an equally comprehensive choice, where every item bore an indication of the amount of water it could throw off in a minute, from the ten-gallon hat upwards. These were especially popular among the American visitors for taking back and outdoing those boasters at home. There was a whole bay full of waterproof underwear and foundation garments, essentially a modified range of inside-out incontinence wear that had been uniquely developed for the island to keep the intrusive weather at bay.

There was a separate bar with rails featuring island sweaters, all hand-knitted by Niamh and her ilk. And off the main area there was a combined snug and fitting room where you could try on any garment, and use the special ensuite high-power shower cubicle to test-drive the garment in anything from a grade 1 drizzle to a force 9 deluge. But what probably made the pub most popular as a rainwear outfitter was the fact that you could also try out the favoured outfit for an evening's drinking - a key criterion since few people on the island bothered to take off these garments when entering the pub.

Upstairs there were rooms for guests to stay in, and downstairs traditional island food was served all day. So Mickey Squigley's was the first place to repair to if you were a visitor. Indeed, you might reach the end of your stay without ever setting foot outside it if the weather was anything like the usual. One way or another, the hydraulic entrepreneur did very well out of it.

Pretty much everyone present on the island, visitors and locals alike, seemed to be in the bar that day in varying degrees of prominence. Among the outsiders, the flamboyant de Boyle clan, who came year after year, was conspicuous. Now they were ensconced with Sir Lancelot and Lady Bryony in command, establishing their aristocratic presence by taking over the showerproof evening wear department, with both sexes eagerly trying on the specially treated cocktail dresses and dinner gowns and getting a little overexcited in the peculiar wetsuit hybrids. The writers of the chemical generation, by contrast, conspired with others of the more hiply inclined in a thick haze of herbal smoke in the remotest of the back rooms.

The bulk of the overseas visitors, summer-school students and fresh-faced nymphs wandered round endeavouring to make sense of it all, and wondering who was important enough to associate with. Deirdre and Modesty were not enjoying themselves, but Sally-Anne appeared to be making useful contacts galore. Angela Blossom was nowhere to be seen, probably intimidated by the presence of Niamh. There was quite a cluster of punters round the most notable European celebrity, the exotic novelist and socialite Gertrude Steiner, rumoured to be the secret lovechild of Rudolf Steiner and Gertrude Stein.

The small clutch of raga-sagateers, on the island for the first time, having once thought themselves now immune to culture shock, stared at it all in bewilderment. The slim poets tried to be noticed, but tended to fade into the shadows owing to their invariably all-black attire and carefully cultivatedly wan and melancholic complexions. The fat American authors of fat American epics consumed fatty snacks to make themselves fatter still. The young Turks got more and more upset as they could find no one prepared to engage with them in an angry exchange. The post-modernists held cryptic, self-referencing deconstructed conversations which no one could understand, least of all themselves. The roving agents, talent scouts, reporters and other low-life gutterati roamed in a predatory manner, homing in on anyone who might be buying a round of drinks.

The locals were out in force too. You could generally spot them for they always kept their rainwear on, since you never knew when you were going to be mortally offended by someone and have to leave in a hurry. Finbar McFogarty discussed the finer points of the likely upcoming programme with Corbel McLintol, the local expert on the romantic novelette. Five generations of the Quillories, the island's oldest family of professional writers, kept their distance from their traditional enemies, the Reame dynasty. Many locals were there that were never seen out at any other time of the year. Most of the island tradespeople were present too, from Bran Moughan the baker to Minty McGinty the hill farmer, who'd brought a couple of Damp-faced Merinos down with him for a bit of a day out, sneaking them a taste of salad from the buffet when Mickey wasn't looking. With most of the locals it was a time for reporting on works in progress, gathering gossip on other folk's projects, starting up rumours that might later become realities, finding someone to help you think of the word you've been trying to think of for the last twelve months, meeting people to base characters on, swapping sub-plots, and other such literary cattle-dealing - all in the context of consuming a vast amount of drink.

Cormac Flannelly was speaking tantalisingly about his new works. Cormac was author of an almost unheard of classic, the book that started the whole cult of writing sequels to novels that you hadn't written yourself. It was called *Catch 23* and was based on his own experiences while experiencing depression owing to not being well known as a writer. The substance of the eponymous *Catch 23*, he is explaining autobiographically to some wide-eyed wannabes, occurs when you get so low and your life is so bad that you reckon it's not worth going on with, so you decide to end it all. But having made that decision you realise that there are all kinds of things that you can now do because you no longer need to worry about the consequences - running up huge bills maybe, or committing terrible but enjoyable crimes. So you embark on an orgy of such activities as a prelude to topping yourself. But then you realise that you're enjoying life again; so you doubt whether you should do yourself in after all, and you put it off and continue to have a great time. However, the consequences of your spree quickly start to catch up with you, and life becomes unbearable again and you become depressed once more, and soon you begin to re-contemplate the unthinkable. It's a tricky one, Cormac explains. He begins to speak of the post-sequels - Catches 24 to 27 - but his listeners have already begun drifting away, having grown restless at his mention of unspeakable but pleasurable crimes.

Even P.Q. Dillinger is here today; a man considered eccentric even on Inishower. He's making his very brief annual appearance, probably just to make sure that he will be talked about in his absence for the next year. Dillinger is far and away the island's best-known novelist, and certainly its most notable recluse. He's abrasively known as PDQ because of his notorious lack of haste in writing. PDQ is an exile from the US, having come here many decades ago to escape attention following the huge success of his debut novel of elusive sexual awakening in a small agricultural community, *Catch Her in the Hay*. He lives far up a narrow winding lane on the deserted northern slopes of the island, and threatens with a shotgun anyone who comes near him. He gets his provisions delivered by helicopter once a year from the mainland; his disposition might be better if he ate more fresh vegetables. PDQ is also the only resident ever to have worn sunglasses. Rumour has it that his fridge is filled with manuscripts for seven further novels that he has completed over the last forty years, which he refuses to show to anyone. Today PDQ stays just long enough to turn down a dozen interviews and be sure that people have pointed him out to one another and muttered about him in sufficient distaste, before disappearing once more up the mountainy lane.

One other attendee at the opening should perhaps be mentioned in the interests of completeness - a shadowy figure lurking in the dark recesses of the underwear department, feigning interest in the 'Last Line of Defence' range of water-repellent Y-fronts, and quite unnoticed by everyone.

Dr. O'Toole passed with pleasure among the company - greeting old friends, pressing flesh in the characteristically limp and damp traditional island manner, accepting tokens of favour from literary personages in return for promises of prominence in the characteristically malleable programme, soaking up adoration from students, and generally basking in anniversarial esteem. As he circulated among the faithful and the not so faithful, part of his mind rehearsed his opening speech. Captain Flaherty drifted along in his wake, taking it all in and not saying much. His attention, too, was divided, for he was also keeping half an eye on the comely form of

Niamh, who was fulfilling her part-time duties as special festivities catering manager at Squigley's.

And the results of Niamh's efforts were now on display in the form of the festival buffet meal, an immense spread of prepared mackerel laid out with garnishings on the great oak table at the back of the main bar. This bounty was set off by the magnificent drapes behind, with their intricate motifs of that favoured fish, executed twenty years before by Molly O'Toole herself for the very first festival. The fillets of maybe two hundred fish had been transmuted by Niamh into the island's favourite delicacy. Preparation of this traditional dish involved marination in rainwater that has been gathered in a thunderstorm and saturated for a month with the essential oils of a cocktail of selected herbs of the bog. The female line of each island family had its own version of this recipe, handed down from mother to daughter since well before anyone could remember; but Niamh's inherited formula was widely regarded as the finest. The doctor had many times tried to winkle the specifics out of his wife and then his daughter on the grounds of cultural and botanical comprehensiveness for his archives, but always without success. After marination, the preparation of the fish is completed by sousing the fillets with high-octane vintage bog poteen, a powerful preservative and anti-oxidant. No cooking is involved. The doctor maintained that it was from Inishower that this technique originally spread around the ancient world, eventually inspiring the Japanese invention of raw fish sashimi.

These delicacies would be tucked into directly after the opening speeches. In the meantime islanders passed by the display, checking its credentials by visual and olfactory means - comparing the colour, texture and aromas with mackerelfests of former years. The results of this assessment were almost universal approval; compliments were paid to Niamh, and the captain too received congratulations on the quality of the piscine components that he had mysteriously provided that morning. Rumours of his likely musicianship were circulating too, and conjectures that he must be a man with more than one story in his head; might the festival be blessed, locals enquired, with some of his melodious or narrative offerings? The captain graciously received the appreciation, but did not commit himself.

Suddenly the doctor was starting into his speech at the front of the bar, and the crowd drifted towards him from all corners and crannies of the establishment. There could be no prouder or more unique moment in a man's life, he was saying (exactly as he had said on every such previous occasion) than this particular festival and this very moment was for him. He was honoured (he reiterated) to be instrumental in the launching of the twentieth annual literary festival of Inishower. He was bowled over (yet again) to be able to play such a part in the island's time-honoured, honour-laden festive tradition. History was in the making, he reassured those present. All and sundry had come from near and far, and he welcomed each and every one - islanders and visitors, old and young, rich and poor, writers and future writers, celebrities and celebrities-to-be. This year's festival would be a veritable cornucopia of talent, a wordfest bonanza on a greater scale than ever before. There would be book launches and readings, competitions and prizes, literary lunches and gala dinners, bookish shenanigans and celebrations of every genre known to man and beast. And that was just the start, the doctor intimated, now getting into his swing. There would be parties and hooleys and *fleadhs*. Nor would there be any shortage of intellectual stimulation, emotional satisfaction or spiritual fulfilment. Heels would be kicked up, whoopee would be made, and wild oats would no doubt be sown in good measure. In short, the crack would be great. And it would all take place in an atmosphere of harmony, fellow-feeling and good cheer, he guaranteed it. And now, without further ado, he said...

"Fire! Fire! The place is on fire!"

The cry came from the back of the bar. Everyone looked round. Flames were leaping from the table of mackerel, and spreading to the heavy ornamental drapes behind them, licking up almost to the ceiling.

Another voice rang out, firm and authoritative. It was Mickey Squigley, the master of moisture. "Get in line, now," he called out as if nothing unusual was afoot, "and pass these along." Ninety-five pints of stout from the top of the bar were quickly passed along a line of variegated helpers and thrown onto the blaze. Ninety four of them seemed to do the job - maybe the bog stout contained some sort of antidote to the fieriness of the poteen - and the last one was snaffled by a seasoned hack. Soon all that remained from conflagration was a blackened mass of smouldering, kipper-smelling carcasses.

While it might be argued that future historians would mark this event out primarily for its accidental discovery of a quite new kind of island delicacy, on this occasion it served mainly to stop the official proceedings entirely in their tracks. Old feuds instantly reignited, and recriminations broke out among those present as to who were the perpetrators of such a vile act, and what were their motives. The Quillories accused the Reames, saying they couldn't stand the likelihood of being eclipsed in the opening events. Cormac Flannelly pointed the finger at Bridie Boru. Bridie Boru blamed Battie McBride, Battie McBride blamed Boxty Falloon, and each member of the de Boyle clan blamed whomever had been sleeping with their own partner most recently. But the rest reckoned it must have been PDQ, and started to form a lynch mob. However, before setting off they decided to have a few drinks to steady their nerves; then they had a few more drinks to get their courage up; and after having a few more drinks for the road they forgot what it was they were steadying their nerves for. So they just stayed on for a few more drinks; for wasn't it a wet old night, anyhow?

Only Captain Flaherty had anything resembling a sensible view on the subject. For his own reasons, he had continued to keep a part of one eye on Niamh as she went about her preparations; and he'd noticed a certain shadowy figure stealthily moving from the underwear department and taking up station behind the curtains at the back of the mackerel table, just after Niamh had done the ritual dousing with poteen. But at this stage the captain wasn't saying anything to anyone.

In the farthest back room, meanwhile, the chemical generation continued absorbing chemicals without the faintest inkling of anything having happened at all.

The Rain

The inhabitants of Inishower have a great range of vocabulary for the various kinds of precipitation that occur on the island; for in this climate the ability to distinguish between them can be a matter of life and death. Indeed, Inishovians use more words for kinds of rain than the Eskimos have for varieties of snow. Articulation of the different sorts encountered on Inishower is certainly a science in itself, yet also a form of poetic expression.

First, the lighter categories of precipitation. These are classically catalogued as follows: a thin drizzle; a damp, humid imminence of rain; a pernicious misty sort of rain; gentle rain like the settling of the mountain dew; an insidious rain that you can't see till you're out in it; a very watery kind of rain; a rain that resembles thin gruel; rain that's more like thick porridge; and almost not raining at all.

At the heavier end of the pluvial spectrum, three basic species of downpour are recognised: a soft, comforting type of a downpour; a fair-to-middling sort of a downpour; and a dreadful drenching downpour. Worse, though, are these: the rain that's too dense to walk through; rain that's solid with no gaps of air between the drops; torrenty rain that would wash you away with all your family; and the rain that's mixed with cats, dogs, mice, rats and assorted livestock.

Other important precipitative categories include snowy rain, sleety rain and rain that falls upwards and gets in under your oxters in a nasty way. There is also a changeable windy rain that is always blowing in your face whichever way you turn.

Specialised rain terminology exists for many other types of precipitation that are encountered only on this island. These include Quarefall, a deceptively dry kind of a rain; Potchoon, a rain that's the colour of bad whiskey; and Bog-Douche, or dirty black rain that smells like rotten herrings. Muldershugh is a sticky, treacly rain, while Ballygowanspume is a pleasant rain that's naturally sparkling and fizzy. Driving Rain on Inishower means rain that can fall on you while you're still inside your car. Spitting Rain has a texture reminiscent of thickish saliva, and Snotburst is self-explanatory. Perhaps most feared of all, though, is the rain that comes in winter with hailstones the size of big potatoes.

U.o'T.

13 Remembrance of Things, Pissed

The following noon Dr. O'Toole and the captain walked down through a heavy downpour to Squigley's bar to see if they could get the festival going again. Sir Lancelot de Boyle and his clan were due for a big set that evening, and that was expected to be a bit of a highlight. Niamh, in her catering capacity, would already be down there. Dr. O'Toole had been affected by last night's events to a degree that had surprised the captain. What he didn't know was that the doctor had sat up half the night studying his archives of orally transmitted lore, paying particular attention to the records gathered from the old-timers of the scryers' traditional interpretations of omens and events. Apparently anything involving accidental incineration of mackerel did not bode well for the coming times.

The captain, by contrast, seemed brighter by the day, and had already been out early in Malachy's boat to bring back a replacement cache of the prized fishes. Going down to Squigley's he still had over his shoulder the boxed instrument which he'd taken out with him in the boat. Malachy had still not shown his face at the doctor's house, though on their way to the venue the two men heard rumours of him; some said that he'd been glimpsed lurking about in the small hours, gaunt and sunken-eyed, by the last of the revellers returning home. Niamh had not reacted well to any hint of questioning.

In Squigley's the regulars were more in evidence than visitors, who by and large were still sleeping off the previous night's skinful. The islanders were reacting to the disturbing events in the time-honoured manner when something of particular magnitude or trauma had happened - by talking incessantly, drinking a great deal, and sublimating the issue in an impromptu musical *sesshun*. So when the two men entered the main bar, they were immediately swallowed up in a roomful of smoke, conversation and solid music.

Mickey Squigley brought them a complementary pint of bog-stout each.

It was like walking into a big tidal swell. The *sesshun* was already in full swing; as was the way, every instrument followed the same lively, rocking traditional tune, and the rhythm of it went straight into the body and being of all present, whether they were listening or not. The crowd was going with the music, but most were conducting passionate conversations as well - analysing the recent turn of events, assessing the prospects for the festival, arguing for the sake of it, and bewailing the lack of mackerel. Listening to the music was done with the physical fabric of the bones and the blood rather than with the ears, which were kept free for the chat even if you could hardly hear the sound of your own voice.

Captain Flaherty felt the music in his blood all right. He watched the musicians in silence. There were fiddles and banjos and *bodhrans* and the odd guitar, mostly played by the younger islanders or by *graighaoeils* that had got up earlier than the others; but what interested him more was the instrument being played by some of the more elderly locals. The doctor noticed his interest, and explained the Inishower Box to him - a kind of concertina with bellows made from the skin of the now extinct island beaver, bestowing unrivalled flexibility and durability in damp conditions. Maybe one day, the doctor quipped, scientists would be able to bring back the local beaver, using genetic material from the gusset of one of those instruments.

After Mickey had brought them another couple of pints each the doctor took off on his rounds - spreading the word about a planned relaunch ceremony in the evening, getting in touch with the mood of the community, hearing views on how bad things were, pointing out how much there was to look forward to and generally re-establishing his entrepreneurial credibility. The captain moved over to a corner where he was surrounded by unusual species of gabardines, and from there immersed himself in the music. The air in the room seemed to reel and sway and swing to and fro with the energy that was in it. As each tune ended there would be a bit of a gap and then, by some mysterious wordless process, a new one would be agreed upon and started up at full tilt, with one collective voice. The body would once more be invaded and thrilled as the music reached into the lungs and the guts, the heart, kidney, spleen and the gizzard, until a similarly mystical unanimity brought that tune to an end. After every five or six sets of lively numbers - jigs or reels or hornpipes, polkas or sundry gadabouts, there would be a change of pace for the slow airs known as the Inishower Dampeners.

When the sixth or seventh of these mellower numbers came around, the captain became restless and stirred from his stillness. After settling for a moment he stirred again, bent down unobtrusively, opened the container at his feet and took out his own instrument. Quietly he began to join in, playing for his own ear more than anything else. Several nearby conversationalists nonetheless stopped talking; and a couple of instrumentalists stopped as well, and several heads turned his way as if wondering were they hearing something or not, coming from in among the gabardines. At this the captain stopped, put down the instrument and raised a pint up in front of his face. The players resumed their playing, and the talkers talked on with full force.

But by the time the next dampener came round the captain had drunk an additional three pints that had appeared in front of him by the anonymous hand of grateful recipients of mackerel, and the bog stout was taking its hold. Now he reached for his instrument again and began to play softly, with his eyes closed. Some musicians near him left off their playing and looked and listened, but the captain was on his way, and this time he played on. More instruments left off playing in mid-bar. Talkers nearby, suddenly able to hear themselves speak, looked round for the explanation of such a conundrum. In this way a slow wave of contagious, osmotic hush spread steadily out from the captain's corner, as more heads heard the sound and turned towards its source. Before long only the captain was left playing.

In a realm of his own, the captain worked the bellows of the exotic device to bring forth its eerie voice. His fingers fell across the ivory keys without apparent connection to the consciousness of his mind, and the plaintive notes spiralled out of the tuskine pipes and into the silent throng. Away at the far side of the bar, the doctor too turned to listen. He studied the music; the sounds defied adjectives, they were difficult to pin down. But the effect was expansive; it wanted to take you somewhere and you wanted to go there. That was it - something to do with yearning, wanting to belong to the music and go to its source, something like that. The doctor alone noticed his own detachment; part of his mind was always observing, recording patterns and details, making mental notes to be written later into archives. Why did he always have to do that? But in the end, even he realised, you had to stop analysing; you forgot to analyse, because wherever you were going, you didn't bring that bit of yourself with you. You were part of the web of sound throughout the room, a network of permeating vibration in which everything was felt throughout the whole structure, with Captain Flaherty at the centre of it.

    The captain, unaware of this, eyes still closed, just played. He took the tune and went into the distance. He took it into other tunes and he took it to places where it wasn't a tune at all. And he took everyone with him; people edged their chairs closer to him, straining to hear better; standing individuals round the bar drifted in his direction in a kind of spontaneous, slow-motion migration, as unarranged as the seasonal travels of animals moved by the seasons. The mass of people in the room were drifting and merging and finding their pole, like iron filings in a magnetic field.

    Niamh, looking in briefly from the kitchen to see why it had gone quiet, was caught by the sound too. Now she stood still by the door; she wanted to retire back into the canteen, but she didn't. She didn't want anyone to see her like this; but she needn't have worried. She stayed a long time, held in the web.

Music like that might have its own sort of time; but every kind of time has its end, and towards the fullness of that time, something began to alter in the sense in the body. It was like being a diver coming up from below after being submerged for a long time; you weren't at the surface yet, but you knew you were on your way. You were coming up for air, returning to base. Maybe you didn't want the dive to end, but it was happening whether you liked it or not. You had to come back from wherever you'd been.

Everyone was coming back. The whole room was getting ready to resurface; it was a matter of agreement now; it was in the collective body. The music was announcing its ending over the web. And then you noticed that you were still hearing reverberations inside, but the music had stopped. What you heard was silence.

Outside, it was dark. The captain was still sitting with his eyes shut. When he opened them, it was to find all other eyes upon him; the audience were silent. They, the people of Inishower, lost for words: it was an unheard of occurrence; there was a new resource to add to the island's mythological database. The fact was undeniable; nothing needed to be said.

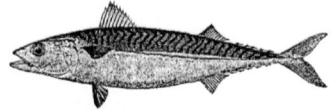

14 Latitude

Pints were raised to lips in silent tribute, savouring the moment; moments are of different length, and this was a long one. Another pint appeared in front of the captain.

Eventually someone spoke up. "Have you a story inside you at all, Captain Flaherty?"

The captain sipped at his pint.

"Ah go on!" said another man.

"Ah you will!" said another.

The captain seemed to ponder the request; he peered into the distance for a long time, as if looking for clues beyond the walls of the pub and the shores of the island, on the horizon and on out over the curvature of the earth. Then he smiled, as if something had come to him; an acceptable solution perhaps. It was a while more, but he did in due course begin to speak in that accent which nobody could quite place.

"There was a young boy once; and this boy dearly loved the sea. Sad to say, though, he lived with his parents right in the middle of a very large country far from any coast; and his parents didn't like the sea; no doubt that was why they lived in the middle of such a very large country. The boy had never even seen the ocean, but he'd read about it in books; in fact he had never read any books other than books about the sea. That was how he knew he loved the sea in the first place; that was where he'd first found out about the sea.

"This young boy was very unhappy, even though his parents loved him dearly and gave him everything that a boy could expect to have. Most of the time, the boy went around in a bit of a gloom, which would only lift a little at odd times such as when he was taking a bath, or when he could stand out in heavy rain getting extremely wet. People didn't understand this; they considered him very strange.

"Naturally the boy's parents worried. They panicked about him being depressed. They fretted over his thinking about the sea all the time. They feared that he would catch a cold from sitting in the bath when the water had gone cold, or from standing out in the rain until he was soaked to the skin.

"Now this particular boy also had strange ways with salt. While all his friends spent their pocket money on sweets and toys and faddish games, he would use his spare cash on buying salt. And he would always keep some salt about his person; he would never go anywhere without a pocket full of it. His mother didn't like this habit because it made his trousers baggy with the weight, and wore out the pockets too.

"And he would put lots of salt on his food. The mother would try to tempt him towards a more balanced diet by saying that he wouldn't get any salt if he didn't eat his greens or pudding, but then he would put salt on his pudding as well. His father wasn't much help, either. He just kept saying that it was just a phase and that the boy would grow out of it, and then he'd go back to reading his newspaper all about what was going on in the middle of their big country, far away from the sea.

"Then the boy discovered that he could imagine he was in the sea by adding salt to his bathwater, and pretend that he was in the middle of seaspray with waves crashing over him by standing in torrential rain and thunderstorms with a big cake of salt on his head; he could taste it running down his face and trickling into his mouth, just like salty seawater. And he even put salt into his pillow so that as he pressed his head onto it, he could hear it scrunching like walking on the beach; and every night without fail he would dream about the sea.

"Every year when summer and school holidays would come, the boy would hope that his parents would take him to the seaside. But his parents enjoyed nothing more than rough hikes in wild mountain scenery; so that's the kind of holiday they'd have, year after year. And anyway, the mother was extremely prone to seasickness; she'd feel a little queasy if anyone so much as asked her to contribute to a lifeboat appeal, which admittedly didn't happen frequently where they lived.

"So each summer the boy would plead with them to go to the seaside for their holidays; but every year they would go instead for rugged hikes in wild mountain scenery. But each year they'd notice that the boy would take more and more salt, and become more strange in his ways. So they got doctors and specialists to come and see him, to find out what was wrong. The doctors would turn up and examine him; they'd find nothing wrong with him, inform the parents that he was in fine health but unusually fond of salt, and go away again.

"One year, as the summer holidays approached, the boy dug in his heels and refused to eat anything at all but salt. After a few days of this, he was getting thinner and thinner and paler and paler and stiffer and stiffer, so his father finally gave in and said that they could go for a short trip to the seaside, in the last week of the holidays. The boy was overjoyed, and in gratitude ate a whole meal without any salt. He didn't sleep at all that night for excitement.

"When the final week of the holidays came at last, they loaded up the car and set off for the coast. The father didn't really have any idea just how far it was, for it wasn't at all his idea of a dream holiday so he hadn't really done any proper planning. It was a very long drive, involving several overnight stays. The boy's mother was seasick almost from the start with the motion of the car, so they had to stop all the time for her to get out and be ill. After three and a half days of sporadic driving, they were still only halfway to the sea; so the father said that there was nothing else for it; they would have to turn round and spend the rest of the week going back.

"The boy was traumatised by this episode. His salt intake went up steeply, and for a month he didn't speak to anyone, except the owner of the delicatessen where he bought his salt supplies. The parents worried all that month; but when fall came he seemed to settle down again, although he was quieter and more brooding than usual. That winter, on his thirteenth birthday, he made a decision. He realised that his parents loved him dearly and had always tried to do their very best for him, but he knew in his heart that it was vital for him to pursue his true destiny in life. He didn't know what that destiny might be, but he was pretty sure that it must have something to do with the sea. So that evening he sat through the birthday party they had thoughtfully arranged for him, with lots of games and decorations and cakes and puddings and vegetables, though with hardly anything at all that had salt in it, and then he went up to his room. He packed a bag with a few essentials - his compass, saved-up pocket money, a big fat sweater, sou'wester hat and a bag of the best quality sea salt - and then lay awake on his bed. When the parents had been asleep for an hour, he wrote a note saying that he loved them very much and appreciated what they had done for him, and hoped that they could understand that it was vital for him to pursue his true destiny in life, even though he didn't know what that destiny might be, and pointing out how futile it would be for them to try to find him because he could have gone in so many different directions, since they had made their home right in the middle of the big country.

"And then he set out for the middle of the town where the roads went in all directions, and he selected one at random and started out walking. After a couple of hours walking he was lucky enough to get a lift in one of those big lorries that puts rock salt on the roads in the middle of winter to stop vehicles skidding; and the driver asked if the boy was hungry, and shared his anchovy sandwiches with him. The next morning he got an even better lift with a long-haul truck doing international transport of kippers. And the driver told him what the sea looked like, and what people did there, and all about the life cycle of the herring and different ways of curing it, and how the salt that his company used was a rare variety of red salt that had to be imported specially from Usbekistan, expensive but well worth the extra cost, and he gave the boy some of the kippers to try, and the boy agreed that they were excellent.

And as they travelled towards the coast the boy grew more and more excited.

"Well at long last, after days and nights of driving and resting and eating the stock from the truck, they reached the port. The lorry driver gave him a couple of packets of best Usbekistani Red Kippers and wished him luck, and dropped him off at the harbour, where his truckload would go off to discerning seafood gourmets all over the world.

"Of course the boy was euphoric. The seaside was just as he had imagined and read about, only more so. The tangy smell of the sea filled his nostrils. The sounds of the gulls thrilled his ears. The sight of the big waves rolling in beyond the harbour filled him with an overwhelming sense of excitement; he could feel the blood tingling inside him. He walked round the harbour, taking it in. He watched the boats going in and out, and the fishermen mending their lobsterpots, and the sailors preparing the ships.

"As he walked along the quays he spotted a strange-looking vessel, nothing like anything he had seen in any book. It seemed older and queerer than the other ships that were in port. It had funnels and propellers and other bits made from metal, but it also had wooden masts and cloth sails and a steering wheel on the deck. Going closer, the boy noticed that there was something pinned to one of the masts; it was a notice, written on a scrap of paper with curled-up edges. 'Cabin boy required', it said. 'Must have inexplicable yearning for the sea. Apply below deck.' "Aha!" thought the boy, and he crossed the narrow plank that led onto the boat. With a mixture of excitement and trepidation, he stepped onto the deck; the boat swayed a little on the gentle roll of the harbour sea. He saw no one, but noticed a small door that seemed to lead down below. The boy made his way through the low opening and descended a narrow, twisting staircase; at the bottom he found himself in a darkened room. The walls were patterned with sliding shadows cast by a fitful candle, as the ship tilted slowly this way and that.

"Suddenly the boy realised that there was someone else in the room. An old man was sitting in the darkest corner, observing him intently. As his eyes adjusted to the gloom, the boy saw that the man had a peaked cap and a leathery, wrinkled face and a bright eye - just the one. In front of him was a table covered in blue sea-maps. The man was scrutinising him.

"'Excuse me, sir,' said the boy. 'I've come about the...'

"'Yes yes yes,' replied the man, in a voice full of tar and driftwood and leathery sea-boots. 'That's a stiff walk you have there, and a bit of a crackle in your joints. Ye've got the job. We set sail at the top of the tide.' At this the captain reached up into the gloom over his head and rang a massive brass bell. The resonance of it shook the boy and the room and everything in it. And from up above, the boy heard the ship immediately spring to life: feet running to and fro on the deck, ropes being pulled, sails unfurling, engines starting up, timbers beginning to creak.

"'This is going to be the journey of your life, boy -' said the captain, '- the like of which you cannot imagine; a journey for which you have already prepared yourself, whether you know it or not. Our quest will take us over the seven seas. It's going to be tough, I can tell you. But you'll be all right as long as you take your orders from me and nobody else. Oh yes.' He paused. 'You needn't bother much with the crew; they're a good-for-nothing bunch of ruffians.'

"The captain paused again, as if wondering whether to say what he did say next. 'But there is one thing, one great danger of which you must be mindful, or it will be the undoing of us all. Oh yes...'"

That evening Captain Flaherty was still speaking. The crowd were still, and the pints were on the table, hardly touched. As with the music, the listening body could tell that things were drawing to a close.

"Finally," the captain was saying, "the ship returned to its home port. But news of the journey and its horrors had gone ahead of them; and upon its arrival, every man-jack of the crew was hanged, drawn and quartered. But the captain and especially the boy - now become a grown man through all that had passed - were feted by the town; the celebrations went on all night. In the morning, he shook hands with the ageing captain, and took his leave.

"For some years after that, he wandered along the coast, joining this ship and that and searching for adventures and ordeals, but nothing was ever quite the same as that first extraordinary episode. Perhaps he realised now that you can never recreate anything that has happened in the past - and that you never need to. And after further years of drifting, he realised that his heart was no longer in this business of seafaring and adventure. It was time to do something else with his life. Indeed, he knew that his lust for the sea and all its ways had finally been satisfied. He was no longer in love with the sea. He became aware that he pined instead for the land-locked regions; and so he set off inland.

"And as time passed, the man found a place to settle down. And he met a woman and they fell in love, and it didn't seem to bother him at all that she experienced a peculiar nausea at any mention of the sea. And he married her, and in time they had a son. And maybe there was something unusual about this boy of theirs from the start, or maybe there wasn't; to tell the truth I can't rightly remember."

It was time to stop.

And in the back room of Squigley's, in among the waterproof hats, the chemical generation carried on with their favourite forms of ingestion, and never heard a word of the story.

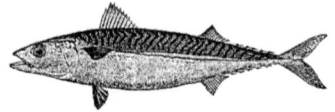

15 Le Boite de Dejeuner Nu

On waking next morning, Dr. O'Toole felt somewhat better. Never mind the omens, the captain's impromptu deliveries of yesterday had put things back on track. Never mind missing out on the planned readings by the de Boyle set; the punters loved the goods delivered. Never mind that the re-launch never happened either; it wasn't the first time that the festival got going without having been started. Anyway, there was no way the doctor could have stopped the thing short even if he'd wanted to. The enigmatic Captain Flaherty was clearly a man of many parts, with a surprising capacity to pull things out of his sleeve; a man of many private parts, you might say.

And the punters wanted more of him - not only the locals, but many of the visitors too had registered their enthusiasm with the doctor, in the drinking that followed late into the night. Not least among the admirers were some of his own masterclass pupils, and not least among these, he noticed, was Sally-Anne Peachley. That was all right, as long as interest in the captain didn't deflect Sally-Anne from her work. Indeed it could be a welcome source of carnal inspiration to her - welcome from the doctor's point of view - a kind of practical exercise that she could report upon graphically in her class projects.

At any rate, the spirit of the festival was back on course, and the doctor's troubles were behind him. It was the first day of festival workshops, and there was a good line-up for entertainments later on in the evening. At the top of the bill was a sampling of works in progress by those bad boys of books, and this would undoubtedly involve a useful bit of controversy. The whole day's action would be at Tadgh McDadgh's, the festival's number two venue.

As he came downstairs the doctor was greeted by the familiar oily aroma of fresh pan-fried mackerel. Captain Flaherty was contentedly tucking into a brace of the desirable creatures. Niamh sat in the corner, knitting a short piece fashioned from thick speckled wool, in a dullish mixture of greens and browns.

"Good morning!" said the doctor.

"Good morning to you," replied the captain through a mouthful of piscine flesh. Niamh went to the pan where a single fish was sizzling.

"That was a grand performance yesterday," said the doctor. "You had them all in the palm of your hand."

"Ah, not at all," replied the captain. "It was just whatever came out."

"Nevertheless...." began the doctor. This was a hard man to fathom, he thought to himself. One minute he's talking the hind leg off a donkey, the next you can hardly get a word out of him.

Niamh served the doctor his fish, then sat down straight away to knit. Now she was muttering under her breath. The two men ate. Presently she pulled the little that she'd knitted off the spindly needles and rapidly unravelled it.

"How's it going, Niamh?" the captain ventured. Niamh let out a stream of violent Inishower oaths traditionally reserved for knitters.

"Not too well, then," the captain observed, and turned his attention back to the plate. Niamh started afresh with the unravelled wool, knitting speedily and without evident contentment.

The doctor watched her. That piece looked like what she'd started working on for Malachy, he reckoned. He wondered why Malachy hadn't been seen in the house for a while now, only he didn't want to risk getting a mackerel clout round the side of the head. He was able to recognise the warning signals; though men learned these things about island women slowly, it seemed to him, in a hit-and-miss, sub-Pavlovian way that would compare unfavourably with a dim poodle. But they did learn, eventually. The Cleft of Inishower helped.

The captain finished his meal. He too thought better than to ask for more. Niamh uttered further obscenities and proceeded to pull apart the dozen or so rows she had just manufactured. Even so, the cleft was still only on a five.

The doctor turned on his chair to face the door as a precautionary manoeuvre. "Is that a bit of Malachy's sweater, by the way?" he asked sweetly.

"It would be, if I could get anywhere with it," replied Niamh. "I need him for a fitting, and now the tension's completely bollixed."

"I haven't seen the man for a day or two now," the doctor continued. "Have you?"

Niamh started knitting again, with less joy than ever. "Not at all. His boat's in the harbour, but he's not been out. And there's no more mackerel now; only the smoked fillets in the warehouse."

The captain spoke up. "I might just go out in the boat and see if I can find any, if Malachy doesn't appear," he offered. The doctor watched for Niamh's response. She stiffened initially and then softened, a manoeuvre he'd seen her mother do when they were courting; it put him in mind of a jellyfish suddenly freezing, then melting.

"It wouldn't do any harm," Niamh conceded after the moment's thaw.

"I'll do that so, tonight," said the captain. "The moon's filling up, and with a bit of luck there'll be fresh fish in the morning. Niamh stiffened back into the contortions of her knitting.

"Good, so," said the doctor, on the lookout for a chance to quit while winning. "I'll be off to McDadgh's to see how things are going for today's programme. Will you go down with me, Captain Flaherty?"

"I will," accepted the captain. "And thanks for the breakfast, Niamh." He got up; his joints were continuing to loosen by the day. The two men stepped smartly out the back into a sleety downpour, closing the door behind them on a fresh burst of profanities as the knitting was unraveled once more.

McDadgh's *Café Bar de la Mer* sat on the other side of the harbour from Squigley's, an appropriate expression of the rivalry between the two establishments and their respective proprietors. It was already a hive of activity when Dr. O'Toole and the captain arrived.

During most of the year, rival factions on the island tended to split along the geo-cultural fault lines separating these two main poles of cultural establishment, Squigley's and McDadgh's. Those who considered themselves more virile - the warlike Reame dynasty and fractious individuals such as Cormac Flannelly and Boxty Falloon - favoured doing their drinking, writing and adventurous eating of bar snacks at McDadgh's, while the more sedate Quillories and many of the island's leading women writers, like Bridie Boru and Batty McBride, were more to be seen at Quigleys. Tadgh's customers had much the better of the writing facilities, but Mickey's crowd would always be far better clad for the weather. However, all this went out the proverbial window in the festival, and everybody went everywhere because nobody wanted to miss anything - least of a bit of literary conflict which was always a possibility at either place. And on this mid-morning at McDadgh's many of the factions were already here. Harsh words were still being exchanged about the fire, and accusations had already been worked into more than one piece of the writer's art. At many small tables the event was passing into local mythology in a variety of formats and genres, from autobiographical novel through kitchen sink drama to impassioned rebel song.

More talked of, but less written about, was the captain's tour de force of yesterday; less had been written because few could quite pin down what exactly had happened, or explain to anyone not there quite why it seemed significant. It was a rare thing indeed for the writers of the island, committed self-conscious observers to a man, woman and child, to forget themselves enough to be unable to write about it afterwards. "You had to be there," was the best that anyone could come up with.

Mention of the captain also brought up the question of Malachy. Where was he? Why hadn't he been seen? All and sundry knew that he was prone to huffs and disappearances, but this was unusual. And more to the point, what about the mackerel supplies? Mind you, the people were saying, the captain seemed to be skilled in that department, and he had a generous streak in him too that was absent in Malachy. Various rumours were swapped and traded, or manufactured on the spot, with sightings reported of Malachy doing unusual things at odd times of night, and coming into the harbour with boatloads of stuff that certainly didn't look like fish. Naturally there was a bit of a buzz about it, but you had to remember that rumour manufacture was the local speciality; the islanders were all comfortable in that no-man's-land, the creative inter-genre space that exists between fiction and non-fiction. The de Boyle set, of course, were in a big sulk at having their scheduled opening gig squeezed out by the captain's extended set; but the doctor promised them something later in the programme. The early part of the day would be taken up with workshops.

The distinctive Inishower workshop programme formed a key part of the festival each year, attended with enthusiasm by locals and sought after by visitors, many of whom had come specially for them. These were workshops for writers who were totally immersed in their work - folks who lived, moved and breathed writing, people who had been to all the run-of-the-mill events on the regular international circuit; these had to be workshops you just couldn't find anywhere else. McDadgh's 'conservatoire' was the ideal venue; as was customary for these events, all the individual café tables were today rearranged into rows like a big class-room, with the workshop facilitator placed behind the bar - the natural position of power and authority in such a space.

Dr. O'Toole now reflected on the great McDadgh's academic events of the recent and distant past, now part of the mytho-legendary fabric of the place - spoken of still, written about often, and inscribed as graffiti on the walls of the establishment's toilets and rest rooms, where much of the best writing was done at the customers' digestive leisure. Last year's hard-hitting seminar by Ailish Dowdy on *How to Survive in a Writers' Support Circle* had been the saving of many participants' careers. Rory Belcher's *Getting Revenge on Rejecting Publishers* had produced tangible results. And from earlier years *Choosing Ink Colour for Longhand Manuscripts* still stood as a benchmark.

Not all events, though, had achieved such straightforward success. *How to Create a Literary Mafia*, almost a decade ago, had been widely misunderstood, leading to ugly incidents and vendettas that lasted to this day. *Writing Great Endings* went on so long that overseas visitors had to abandon it to catch the last boat home. And last year's keynote event on *Surreal Storymaking*, billed as a presentation from the late Flann O'Brien channelled via the literary psychic Nuala Spigott, had a decidedly mixed reception; for all that came through was a half-peeled banana. Most delegates were disappointed at this, and a few did considerable damage to the establishment - a development that Tadgh approved of - while others went away quite inspired. *How to Stop Writing* had been a total flop. And every year the scheduled symposium by P.Q. Dillinger titled *Becoming a Literary Recluse* had to be postponed because he never showed up to give it.

But that was all water under the bridge; this year's events were completely sold out. Over the next week or two, Sir Lancelot and Lady Bryony would be running a mini-conference on *Starting a Literary Cult*; Bouncer McCall would present a seminar on *Writing Very Heavy Books*, including a special muscle development programme; and this year's *New Genre* slot would be filled by celebrity culinary authoress Filo O'Shea introducing *Crime*

Cookbooks. Today's big workshop, *Displacement Activities for Writers*, was just getting under way; the place was packed to the gills. Inishower festival was once more delivering the goods you couldn't get anywhere else. Dermott Leery was in the full flow of his enthusiastic introduction.

"There's tons of stuff available out there," he was saying, "on how to write better - there's books, courses, videos, cassettes, personal coaching - you name it. But information on *not* writing is a sorely neglected topic." Dermott paused and looked round for acknowledgement; there were nods of agreement from locals, and one or two glances of slight bewilderment from newcomers.

"After all," Dermott continued, "*not writing* is a crucial part of being a writer. All truly great writers spend more time not writing than they do writing; it's obvious, isn't it? And I assert that this is the key to their success." Further agreeing nods and bewildered glances.

"Yet most writers still feel bad when they're not writing. This, of course, is a big mistake. Not-writing is essential to the writer's life; it's what informs the writing itself; it's the source. But the crucial question is exactly how to go about not-writing. The truly great writer does great writing *and* great not-writing. That is what distinguishes him or her from the rest." Nods throughout the audience signify familiarity with aforesaid greatness.

"That's right. I'm telling you, recognition of this phenomenon is going to be the next big thing in literature. It's long overdue. It's going to be hot. We mustn't ignore this profound source of creativity and literary achievement. So let's look now at how we can all develop this aspect of our work. Let's try out some examples of alternative activities." And the rest of the afternoon was taken up with Dermott's comprehensive presentation of hands-on practical displacement exercises for writers.

McDadgh's was the perfect venue for that evening's entertainments. A couple of locally connected authors would do the warm-up honours before the main act, a tour-de-force by the young Turks - Brad Saltfish and the 'bad boys of books', as the doctor liked to call them. Dr. O'Toole cast his eye round the main bar. Niamh was dispensing bar food, for in her spare time she operated in catering mode here too. There was a good crowd, and more people arriving by the minute. Captain Flaherty wasn't to be seen; probably he'd be along presently.

The warm-up readings were already under way. Fliuchan ni Baisteach, a respected and influential Inishower writer, delivered an extract from her new work, a metaphysical crime thriller in which the rain is the murderer. Fliuchan was followed by Hector Conchobhar Earwigger, a self-styled émigré who was now a prominent member of the university establishment in the States. He was a tiny man with dry sallow skin, heavy academic tweeds, ornate spectacles and an unfeasibly high forehead. Hector may have been physically small but he had the aspirations of a literary giant, and saw himself as the natural successor to James Joyce, which was probably why Tadgh was happy to host him. Everything about his writing was big. His ideas were big. His stories were big. His characters were big. He used big words and big punctuation marks and big phrases; most of his major works were all one sentence. That was why he had left Inishower - it was too small for him. And the biggest place he could think of to go was the USA. Of course he had also changed his name - formerly Jo Flynn - to a bigger one.

H. C. Earwigger's work was not terribly well-liked on Inishower, for he had spurned the island and its culture. But his visits were always popular with the stateside visitors; and Inishower fathers would bring their sons to his gigs to highlight the dangers of leaving. For Earwigger now lived in Arizona, and precipitation almost never featured in his writing; the locals liked to quip that "the stream of his consciousness must have dried up". In North America his work sold like hot cakes, especially among the campus literati and academics of the Joycean analysis industry. Tadgh was always keen to have him back every year; and the tastes of the American clientele played an increasingly influential part in the shaping of the island festival with every year that passed. The doctor had to think about these things. And today the wishful writers of big books at their little tables were loving it.

As Hector drew his self-congratulatory reading to a close, in walked Captain Flaherty with Sally-Anne Peachley not far behind him. The doctor noticed it, and he wasn't sure that he liked the interest she seemed to be taking in the man. But maybe she'd heard about the reputation of McDadgh's and was hoping to be violated *à la Hemingway*. Either way, he caught Niamh looking their way as well, in the middle of serving the dried mackerel crisps that were so popular as a snack.

But now it was time for the doctor to announce the next item. He walked to the front with a mischievous twinkle in his eye. And that was when he introduced Brad Saltfish and the Bad Boys of Books. That was when Brad's little embarrassment happened. And that was when Corbel McLintol, Finbar McFogarty and Liam Scroggarty were out in a flash, to see the splinters of wood still falling out of the sky, and the waves still splashing round the harbour .

"I'd say that'll have been Malachy's boat," said McLintol, a man with a good knowledge of carpentry and the behaviour of wood under stress.

"Sure, who'd want to blow that up?" asked McFogarty.

"And more important," says Liam Scroggarty, "where's our mackerel going to come from now?"

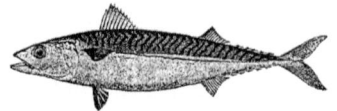

16 A Midsummer's Wet Dream

Dr. O'Toole didn't sleep much that night. But when he did, he manifested a seemingly interminable dream in which he was the ring-master of a vast circus; and the show was not going well. The audience, seated far away at the edges of a great tented space, consisted of the current visitors to Inishower plus all their friends, families and pets. Niamh and her mother were putting on a daring tight-rope act without a safety net, and kept encouraging volunteers from the audience to join them on the high wire. The doctor ran round, endeavouring to fix an old fishing net in place below them, but the enthusiastic volunteers were falling through it and lying in broken heaps on the circus floor; they each looked the doctor squarely in the eye as they fell to their deaths.

The other acts were presented by locals, too. Corbel McLintol rode round the edge of the ring in a chariot with blades coming out from the wheels, attempting to dice anyone who got in the way. Bran Moughan did magic tricks that resulted in the appearance of thousands of loaves of mouldy bread. Someone was training a colony of giant performing ants, which ran riot and ate into the tent poles. The murky figure of Malachy Moodie flitted in and out of the shadows, surreptitiously releasing lions, grizzly bears and other dangerous animals into the arena; then the doctor noticed that the tent was on fire. He endeavoured to distract the audience's attention from all this by doing a contortionist act in which he bent over backwards to make a circle of himself, but was only booed for his troubles.

As the show continued, a group of smartly dressed insurers and financial backers swarmed into the ring and encircled the doctor, demanding that he cancel the show. Captain Flaherty watched from the edge of the ring, looking concerned; the doctor wanted to ask him for help, but found he could not speak in any language that the captain would understand. Eventually the whole arena, with the circus acts, suited entrepreneurs and audience, began to revolve round the doctor as he stood in the centre, with everyone yelling at him to do something. Now it was getting unbearably hot and smoky, and difficult to see anything. The whole thing turned faster and faster still, spinning away until the doctor grew dizzy, lost his balance and felt himself falling, with a distant cry ringing in his ears, "You'll never run a circus in this town again..."

The doctor woke suddenly in his bed, bathed in sweat. It was morning, but a thick dark downpour blotted out the sky and ran down the window in a treacly wash. With relief the doctor realised that the circus wasn't real; yet it soon dawned on him that reality wasn't much better. He lay on in bed, not wanting to get up; but there was a masterclass to get on with this morning. Maybe his nymphs would cheer him up - some of them, anyway. He got dressed and went downstairs.

Niamh was in the kitchen; she hadn't slept well, either. The captain was still asleep. The doctor didn't want any breakfast; he was applying his fail-safe strategy of trying not to think about anything that was problematic. Neither spoke what was on their minds.

But as the doctor walked over to the library through the mucky downpour he could not keep unwelcome thoughts out of his head. First of all the fire, and now this explosion - who was behind it? What were they up to? Was it some disenchanted festival participant with a grudge against him? Surely it wouldn't be any of the islanders, bad as some of them were. Could it be Flaherty's doing? He had been inside McDadgh's at the time of the blast; nonetheless, he could have set it up beforehand. That's right - he'd disappeared for a while earlier on. In fact, all this trouble had only started since the captain had appeared. Was his arrival such an accident of timing? Why was he really here? Was he really as vague as he seemed?

The doctor's masterclass helped to take his mind off things once he'd stopped the students gossiping about the events of the night before, and set them to their work. It was session four of the *Writing Hot Sex* series, entitled *Bringing Erotic Fantasy to Life*. Indeed many of the students produced excellent project work this time. Modesty Thinkwell had perked up and got writing, perhaps benefiting now from immersion in the ambience of the island; though sadly the results shown at this stage were more literary than carnal. Deirdre O'Dowdy was loosening up too, starting to deliver the goods and showing a distinctly healthy hormonal component in her work. But no one was getting close to Sally-Anne Peachley. Her lurid, graphically detailed and compelling work today was very much to the doctor's satisfaction. On re-reading, however, he noticed that the description of the general physical characteristics of the owner of the penis which Sally-Anne had put to such imaginative and exotic use in her piece seemed to bear an uncanny similarity to those of Captain Flaherty. The doctor had mixed feelings about this, despite his admiration for the neat line of speech given to her female protagonist upon the arrival of the Captain Flaherty look-alike, in a piece that was distinctly short on dialogue: "Is that a mackerel in your pocket, or are you pleased to see me?"

After class the doctor was left once more with that overwhelming sense of lost control. He trudged homewards with a heavy tread, and spirits unlifted by pocketed classwork that would normally have him skipping back in eager anticipation of reassessment in the usual personal and very physical way. The rain was falling in great thick ladlefuls as if from some great soup tureen, and that didn't help either. The only thing he could think about was the threat to his beloved festival. Maybe it would be best to bring the whole business into the open, and start by tackling the captain about it straight away.

As the doctor approached the house he noticed his habitual physical response to doing things he didn't want to do; he would describe it as a radical tensing of the posterior trapezius muscles of the neck which transferred pressure to the *semispinalis capitis*, thus restricting flow of blood in the carotid artery and air in the trachea.

It was a classic writer's complaint, something he'd treated a thousand times on Inishower; but in his own case he knew it embodied a lifelong response to walking into any room that contained his wife or his daughter with a mackerel in the hand - a common enough occurrence in view of what each of them thought of his so-called masterclasses.

As he entered through the back door he heard the musical strains of the captain's instrument floating down the hallway from the surgery. Niamh was in the kitchen, knitting. To the doctor's surprise, her brow seemed relatively unfurrowed, even if her demeanour was not the happiest. She was knitting, but she was not swearing. A fine fire was burning in the black stove - a not inconsiderable achievement in itself in the prevalent conditions on Inishower. The air in the room was warm; it seemed thinner, less dense, easier to walk into than was customary. Something unusual was happening. The posterior trapezoids eased. Just for a moment it felt like he was in a room with a potential ally rather than a tormentor.

"Hello Niamh," ventured the doctor.

"Hello," replied Niamh, without looking up from her knitting.

"What do you make of all this, then?"

"Terrible," said Niamh.

"Have you seen Malachy yet?"

The knitter's cleft reappeared. "I have not," said Niamh. "Nobody has." She looked away out through the window.

"I'll go and have a chat with the captain," said the doctor. "I think I hear him in the other room."

"So you do," said Niamh. She turned towards the music, then resumed knitting. The cleft eased a bit.

The doctor walked up the hallway and quietly opened the surgery door. The captain sat on the daybed, playing the contraption with eyes closed. The doctor studied him. Was this the visage of a terrorist, he wondered? He continued to watch and ponder, and next thing he was going with the music and all his thoughts scattered.

After a time he decided to interrupt, and coughed aloud. The captain looked round; his face brightened out of the sobriety of the playing.

"Dr. O'Toole. How are you?"

"Ah, you know. Fair to middling. Could be better."

"I know," said the captain. "It's a bad thing, isn't it? And you wouldn't know what's going to happen next..."

"I was wondering if I might have a word with you," said the doctor. The neck muscles were kicking in again.

"By all means," said the captain. "There's something I want to mention to you as well. Can we go out of the house, though?" The doctor wondered what that other something might be.

"Let's go out on the bog road," he said. The captain got up and put the instrument away. The doctor walked back down the hallway and stuck his head into the kitchen. Niamh was still knitting by the fire.

"I'm just taking a walk," said the doctor; "- with the captain." Niamh gave the look of one who wonders what's up.

"We'll be back soon," said the doctor. In point of fact, they wouldn't be back soon.

As the two men stepped outside the rain was easing off, not much more than a light downpour; you could almost see the vague mass of Mount Eireaball away in the distance. They started out on the bog road and walked a while in silence, looking out over the drenched landscape. There was no doubt that the captain was making a spectacular recovery; he was walking now like a native-born islander. The rain splashed into the surface of the pools of water that lay below the turf banks, stirring up their blackness. But the marsh sparrows chattered in the branches of the wet-thorn bushes, a sure sign that it would brighten up; and the sogweed, whose flowers open only for the very wettest of conditions, were waiting for another day to display their rare beauty to the world. The captain deferred to the doctor's prerogative to initiate conversation. The doctor wondered how to begin.

"Do you know much about explosives at all?" he finally asked, as if on a nothing-to-do-with-anything impulse; he looked straight ahead, but watched for tell-tale reactions with peripheral vision.

"Ah no," replied the captain. "You'd be wanting somebody else for information such as that. The nearest thing I could help you with would be opening a bottle of stout that's been shaken about too much." He smiled, then paused. "What is it you need to know?"

"I need to know who's blowing things up and setting fire to things and goodness knows what next," said the doctor with some vexation.

"Ah yes," replied the captain. "I was wondering about that myself." He paused again. "Tell me, by the way," he went on, "what does your man Malachy look like?"

"Malachy? He's a young fellow, black hair; stoutly built creature, pale skin, bad posture. You'll usually recognise him by the big chip he carries on his shoulder; I don't think Inishower suits him."

"I see what you mean. Is Niamh in love with him, do you think?" ventured the captain.

"Hard to say," said the doctor. "She certainly was at one time, but that was years ago. I think he killed it off with his geurning. But the two of them still carry on anyway; he brings in the mackerel, you know. Or used to, anyway. But Inishower's no place for a man like him if you ask me."

"How do you mean, exactly?" The captain seemed keen to pursue the matter.

"Malachy is no writer; I don't think you'd ever see him so much as pick up a book. And he can't take the rain. When you're like that, Inishower grinds you down; I've seen it before. He'd be better off doing something different, somewhere else." The doctor permitted himself a wry smile. "...Like selling ice creams in the Sahara desert, perhaps." Then he looked at Captain Flaherty. "But why do you ask?"

"Oh, it's just that I saw someone like that the other day," the captain replied.

"You saw Malachy? Where did you see him?"

The captain hesitated, reluctant to say more.

"It's all right," the doctor said. "I won't mention it to Niamh. So where did you see him?"

"Well now, I can't be sure, but I thought it might have been him that I saw at Squigley's on the night of the fire."

"At Squigley's? I didn't know Malachy was there. I'm sure I'd have seen him. Anyway, it wasn't his kind of evening."

"The person I'm thinking of didn't want to be seen," said the captain.

"And you think it might have been Malachy?"

"Well if it wasn't him it was someone with a similar black mood on him."

"There isn't anybody else with that kind of mood," said the doctor. "It would have to be him. What was he up to?"

"I think I'd better not say any more," said the captain, and seemed to mean it. The doctor was thinking. Malachy lurking in the bar before the fire, and now his boat gets blown up. It was a strange conundrum all right.

The two men walked on in silence as the road turned round to the north with the Fishtail Mountain straight ahead of them. The wind had turned to the south; the marsh sparrows and the sogweed were right, and the rain was thinning out by the minute; both mist-shrouded peaks could now be discerned.

The silence served a purpose. To his own surprise the doctor began to ease into the occasion; the old familiar pleasure of walking the bog road and the sense in the landscape that all was as it should be, began to work their way into his system as they always had in the past. He felt something else too, something less familiar - an ease in the presence of another human being, a kindredness of spirit. That feeling might well be at odds with the circumstances, for here he was walking with the man whose arrival had marked the start of things going wrong; but it was there nonetheless. Maybe it was okay. Maybe he didn't need to worry about the captain. Maybe he didn't even need to be entirely in control of things. Maybe there were more important things in life than the festival. Was that possible? No, that was gong too far...

"What do you make of Niamh?" the doctor asked suddenly.

"Ah, Niamh!" the captain laughed. "I'd say there's nobody cooks a finer mackerel on the bone."

Very diplomatic, thought the doctor. "She's all right in her own way you know," he said, "even if she has a tongue on her like an Inishower knitting needle, and could give you a clout like an ass's kick..." The doctor was going to say more, but decided to leave it at that. They walked on; the weather opened up into a delightful light drizzle and the mountain was ahead of them in all its hazy splendour. And the doctor could not resist the feeling of rightness that was coming out of it all; try as he might, he could not at that moment bring himself to worry about the village and the festival and the visitors and the programme and the performances and the troubles, or anything in that line. There were no further demands on his time until the evening, and for the rest of the afternoon it seemed perfectly acceptable not to be in control. In that timeless landscape through which they walked, he thought of nothing that was in the future; his consciousness was suffused with the spirit of the ever-living past. And as they walked on, it seemed the most natural thing in the world to relate to the captain some of the most ancient and little-known lore of the island that he had in his possession.

The Oldest Times

The ancient history of Inishower is shrouded in deeper mystery than even the twin peaks of Sleabh Lasc Eireaball itself; but as with that illustrious monument, we are occasionally afforded brief glimpses and insights into the arcane secrets of the past which this enigmatic island holds.

It has been consistently believed by successive inhabitants of the island that Inishower represents the last remaining fragment of the lost continent of Atlantis, known to have been situated somewhere in the Atlantic between Europe and the Americas. And these civilisations have all possessed an awareness that conventional historians have studiously avoided: that Atlantis was first and foremost a literary empire - an empire ruled by the pen, and probably the first power on earth to recognise the supremacy of that weapon over the sword.

Atlantis was, of course, an extremely advanced technological society; yet its hegemony was spiritual, overseen by a very powerful elite of shaman-priests. These individuals had mastered magical influence over the future through a ritualised form of trance writing known as scrudging, *which they pursued in deep underground chambers. This obscure technique employed as ink an intense electric blue mineral fluid known as* Oleum, *which the Atlanteans had discovered in great reserves that lay deep in the rocks below their city, and which flowed up to the surface under its own pressure when they drilled into it. The fluid was composed of the bodies of trillions of microscopic flying creatures from a far earlier and still uncharted era in the earth's history, transformed by aeons of heat and volcanic activity into a highly charged organic catalyst of* molecular transformation. The art of scrudging was so highly developed among these Atlantean practitioners that they could make anything they wanted happen by simply writing it. If they wanted to go out and defeat an enemy they'd scrudge that, and so it would be. If they wished to repel an attack, they'd write that the attack was successfully repelled; or they might even decide that the attack never happened, in which case their attackers would find themselves inexplicably turning round and going home with a lot of explaining to do. Or if they wanted nothing to happen they'd write that, and take the rest of the day off. And these shaman-priests could live as long as they wanted.

In the end they thought they'd go for all-out world domination. It all seemed very easy; but once they'd got that, it went to their heads and they didn't know when to stop. Now that the whole world was their empire they got drawn into working round the clock, scrudging copiously detailed instructions for how everything was to be in different parts of their colonies. All this, of course, required huge supplies of oleum, and so they needed to drill down into the still greater reserves that they knew lay deeper down in the earth's crust.

This turned out to be disastrous. Under the immense pressure and heat at these levels in the volatile substrata, vast torrents of super-heated oleum began to gush forth, engulfing the chambers where the shaman-priests were engaged in their rituals, swallowing up the city, and flooding out over Atlantis until virtually the entire continent was covered to a great depth in the blue liquid. The dense mineral content of this immense bulk of fluid bore down over the whole area, and gradually the continental plate began to tilt and sink, until the ocean of electric blue eventually mingled with what is now the Atlantic. As pressure was released the flow finally stopped; but now all that remained above the waves of the great range of Atlantean mountains were the twin peaks of what is now known as Fishtail Mountain, tipping up at the western edge. Atlantis had lived by the pen, and now seemingly it had died by the same means.

Yet certain key vestiges of Atlantean culture may still be discerned on Inishower to this day. Local writers use an archaic inverted sinistral writing style that is found nowhere else in the world. Electric blue is still the most favoured colour of ink. And it is said that the practice of scrudging still survives among some of the older islanders who live on the lower slopes of Sleabh Lasc Eireaball; traces of Atlantean genetic residue are undoubtedly to be found among them. The great deluge of oleum ushered in the dampest of times, and it seems reasonable to suppose that only those most resistant to damp would have survived it; and who in the world is more impervious to the ingress of moisture than the pure bred Inishovian?

It is considered by many that certain garment making techniques of the old empire still survive on Inishower. The classic knitted garment for writers, the Scrivlin, is strongly believed to be of Atlantean origin. Of all this we can never be sure, however; for sad to relate, the manuscript of the definitive work on this subject - Knitting Patterns of Atlantis, by Molly O'Toole - was sadly destroyed in a fight with a rival knitter; an irony that the ancient literary shaman-priests of Atlantis could not have written better themselves.

U.o'T.

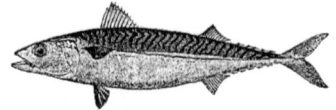

17 Rubberdance

Dr. O'Toole and Captain Flaherty arrived home to find Niamh still knitting in the warm kitchen. She was working quickly and smoothly on something very different from the piece that she'd been working at the day before; the wool was much thicker, the texture richer and the colours a vibrant mix of black, green, blue and white rather than the dull, earthy shades she'd been employing earlier.

"Is that Malachy's sweater?" asked the doctor.

"It is not," replied Niamh with tight-set lips.

"What's for dinner?" the doctor risked.

"Nothing," replied Niamh. "I'll have to go up to the warehouse on the hill to get more of the cured fillets." She paused. "It's a bad thing," she continued. "- a very bad thing that's happening. We're having to start into next winter's stocks already. If you ask me, it's the curse of St. Scombrel." There was nothing the doctor could say. Oh well, he thought, at least there'd be nothing for her to clout him round the head with, for the time being.

Niamh continued knitting. Then she stopped, looked at the captain for a moment, turned back to the work, counted up the rows accumulated so far, and continued. The Cleft of Inishower was on a rating of about three, the doctor estimated; not an all-time low, but certainly a relatively safe level. Then out of the blue it deepened again, to about a seven or so.

"I've been up to Malachy's house on the mountain," she said. That was unusual, the doctor thought. She never went up there; Malachy would always come down to the village. He didn't like anyone going up there and snooping around.

"And was Malachy there?" asked the doctor.

"Not a bit of him. The place was in a mess. Worse than usual. The roof's about to fall in. I reckon he's not been there at all." From the way she spoke, the doctor wondered how much she cared.

"Where has he been then, do you think?"

"Maybe he's sleeping rough," said Niamh.

"But you know how he hates the rain…"

"I know. Or maybe he's over on the mainland."

"Not without his boat, surely," said the doctor. They both glanced towards the captain, who said nothing. Nobody spoke for a minute or two.

"We'll go down to Squigley's for the evening's action," said the doctor eventually. "Will you pop down later on yourself, Niamh?"

"I suppose I will, when I get back from the warehouse. People will be wanting something to eat."

"Would you bring your musical contraption along?" said the doctor to Captain Flaherty.

"I will indeed." The captain went off to the surgery and came back with his battered box. It helped before; maybe it would again, the doctor thought.

Now there was a muckier shower wafting down out of the darkening sky, as they stepped out of the house. There'd be more rain than this before the night was out, the doctor felt sure; and indeed the rain grew heavier as they walked. On the way down to the harbour he spoke to the captain of something else that was on his mind. He related how the Inishower festival also embraced the ancient festival of St. Scombrel, the patron saint of the mackerel, which fell the next day. It was a very bad time for all this trouble to be happening. St. Scombrel's was the most important day of the whole Inishower calendar. And then there was the question of St Scombrel's curse....

But now they were at Mickey Squigley's, and the captain would have to wait to hear more. Squigley's was already full; after all, there was no shortage of stuff to talk about. The locals provided the most vocal presence, but plenty of the visitors were there too. And the gutterati were cleaning up, having discovered that Inishovians were at their highest potential for buying rounds when something untoward had happened. Not one of the young Turks was in evidence.

Mixed glances greeted the doctor as he entered, but he moved round the main bar to see what he could find out, particularly with respect to Malachy. It had been verified that no bits of the man had been found among the wreckage of the boat, or stuck to the outside of McDadgh's building. But was Malachy involved in this at all? Had he left the island? Had he met with an accident? Was he lying somewhere, drowned with the rain? Rumours about him abounded, though on Inishower that meant nothing; mostly these involved the briefest of sightings, more than one source describing him as a thin, wild and demented creature with rampant hair and tattered clothing of the backwards-through-hedge-dragging variety. But any degree of narrative uniformity or harmonisation of detail probably only meant that the relevant rumour-bearers had been drinking together.

Nobody seemed to believe that Malachy was at the bottom of the troubles. Most of the locals would far rather suspect their traditional adversaries, from Tadgh McDadgh and Mickey Squigley with their long history of impuning one another in order to ruin the rival's business, down through the island's hierarchy of ancient epic squabbles. There were one or two new suspects on the agenda, too - Filo O'Shea was one of these, as she was widely known to be researching a new thriller-cookbook based around seafood and terrorism. More important by far, though, than any concern people had about possible danger to life and limb seemed to be the question of the mackerel crisis. There was no fresh fish, no Malachy, no boat for anyone to go out in; and now they were eating into the vital stock of winter preserves - it was serious, all right.

Yet it took more than this to stop Inishovians in their tracks and deflect them from their literary pursuits. They were still responding to trials and tribulations with their customary methods of processing trauma - gossip and speculation, accusation and blame, drinking a great deal - and writing about it all. The collective literary impulse was still the most powerful component in the island psyche; this was never in doubt. The show would still go on; the doctor knew he could take comfort in that, for the time being at least. And they could always fall back on a bit of therapeutic music making; many had brought their instruments, and a restorative *sesshun* might be on the cards.

The show did go on, even if most of the seats by the seaward windows of Squigley's remained empty, and several groups had ensconced themselves safely amongst hanging batteries of heavy-duty rainwear. First up tonight was a reading from the local author Ebenezer Progue, a thin unhealthy man of strikingly sallow complexion and hair actively falling out, even as he read from his work. His eyes rolled permanently upwards in an unnerving manner, and his eerie voice, if not from beyond the grave, sounded like it might soon be coming from that vicinity.

Eb Progue was a relatively obscure author even by Inishower standards, labouring in a somewhat individualised horror genre of his own creation. His work had an affectionate cult following, however, among the handful of residents of Grusen Wood where Eb himself lived. His novels weren't recommended bed-time reading for the kids. They were decadent, crumbling baroque structures haunted by dark brooding presences; as you read your way through them you had the unsettling sense that great heavy, dangerous chunks of story were tumbling down behind you, leaving a trail of destruction and the feeling that next time you might not be so lucky. The individual sentences themselves were long, suffocating and convoluted; they clambered over the stories as ivy does over an ancient tree - parasitically robbing it of nourishment, strangling and ultimately killing it, yet in the end holding the whole structure up even after the content within has become a rotting carcass. Needless to say, no publisher could be found by Progue; nor could any vanity press be persuaded to take it on, even for ready cash. So Ebenezer fashioned the books himself by hand with a primitive press and bindery in a tiny shed at the back of his hovel in the woods.

Progue spoke of his work without any sign of life-force or vitality. Death, decay and the ultimate futility of human existence, he was saying - these were the underlying themes of his work. In truth, the doctor knew, his novels simply suffered from an extreme version of a problem that afflicts any number of authors: the books were very well done, a tour de force even, but nobody enjoyed reading them. Except, of course, the handful of residents from Grusen Wood. Indeed, it was rumoured that persistent attempts to read the work had resulted in unwholesome illnesses and at least one death. Yet Ebenezer reckoned that writing these tomes was his destiny; a writer had to write what a writer had to write. Besides, if he didn't do it, no one else would - there were nods of agreement all round on that.

The doctor himself considered Eb's work a fine example of the marriage of form and content but had been careful not to read it too extensively himself, having treated some of the patients that had. Nonetheless, as festival organiser he was keen to include such curiosities; not for nothing was Inishower festival renowned worldwide for its inclusivity. No other festival could match writers like Eb Progue, even if they wanted to. But even on Inishower, nobody wanted Eb to go on for too long; the power of the work was so pervasive that you could already see listeners going pale and heading for the bathroom. Inclusivity was all very well, but nobody minded when Eb decided to stop and head back to the woods to work on his next major opus.

Ebenezer was followed by Chancer McKeane, a clandestine guest whose story the doctor felt would go down well on Inishower. McKeane sported a beard, dark glasses and cultivatedly nondescript garb, and for good reason. He was here to tell how he'd created a sensation in the publishing world some years earlier. He'd already spent decades churning out well-crafted, workmanlike novels which were universally rejected by all the major publishing houses on the grounds of lack of commercial appeal; none felt that they could market them on a sufficiently massive scale. So one day in a fit of pique McKeane decided to burn the entire plethora of manuscripts, and adopt a completely different tack. He hatched a scheme that centred on the concept of putting marketing before the quality of the work itself; his idea was to 'disappear' in mysterious and newsworthy circumstances leaving behind lots of carefully manufactured, juicy rumours, as well as friends and family who were equally mystified by his disappearance, and an unpublished manuscript of breathtaking blandness and mediocrity. The ploy paid off; an agent was brought in to manage his 'estate', and a bidding war began between several of the largest international publishing conglomerates. In the end the successful bidder paid so much for the book that they were obliged to fork out even more on promotion in order to get their advance back. With this kind of backing, of course, a book's chances of success are very much enhanced; and in that sector of the market, too, blandness and mediocrity worked very much in the book's favour. With careful grooming and a meticulously orchestrated nine-month long lead campaign it became an instant 'shock bestseller'. It did extremely well in hardcover, then fared even better in paperback. A leading bland-and-mediocre Hollywood star liked it, and movie rights were sold. Merchandising plans got under way.

Then the problems began. A couple of reasonably successful spin-off titles were squeezed out of the project - the unauthorised autobiography of the enigmatic late author, the book of the making of the movie, that sort of thing - but more of the real stuff was desperately needed, and heads would roll if it wasn't found. Meanwhile McKeane had clandestinely contacted the publishers and let them know that he was still around; whereupon they made him one of those offers that you simply can't refuse. They all came to an arrangement: a prequel would be 'discovered' and quickly published. A major promotional campaign was immediately instigated for this volume even as McKeane simultaneously wrote it, blander and more mediocre than the first. The book was an even greater worldwide success than its predecessor, its launch coinciding with the appearance of the movie of the first volume.

Then the pressure really set in. The publishers now wanted a new seven-book, seven-movie deal, comprising a further series of miraculously unearthed prequels that each pre-dated the last, each blander and more mediocre than ever. It was turning into a right old mess. In the light of the backlog of deception to date, McKeane's hands were tied; there was no going back now. But at least he didn't have to make public appearances; after all, he had disappeared and didn't even exist.

And so in due course, McKeane related, he wrote the seven additional books, co-operated in seven screenplays, and had seven nervous breakdowns - and still couldn't go home. He was so rich that he spent half his time fearing for his life and the rest worrying about how to spend all the money. The publishers gave him a whole new identity but it wasn't quite the same. And now, Chancer told his enthralled audience, he longed for the good old days when he was a failure and all his manuscripts were rejected, when there was no pressure, when he could do just what he wanted even if he didn't have any money.

It was a salutary lesson and it went down well with the audience, though not necessarily in the manner planned; for it appealed most notably to the bland and mediocre failures present, and those who had achieved nil recognition or fame; not because they felt any better about being this way - they didn't - but because they could now fantasise that they too might suddenly be plucked from oblivion and subjected to the unbearable torment of blockbusterdom, success and wealth beyond their wildest dreams. After all, nervous breakdowns and abject misery weren't so bad; anything was worth putting up with to achieve recognition and success. These individuals felt uplifted and inspired, ready to go away and plumb new depths of mediocrity in their work. On this note of elation the doctor decided to announce a break, and went off on his rounds again. And in one of those unanimous acts of spontaneity, the music started up.

Despite any upliftment arising from Chancer McKeane's contribution, the tune that they struck up reflected the underlying mood of the community. It was one of the oldest and saddest of Inishower's own traditional melodies: a simple, slow air called the Mackerel's Lament. It was a song without words that had grown up for use when the fish had not appeared or could not be caught, reflecting the local belief that the soul of the mackerel itself was suffering in some way. And if the fish suffered, the people would suffer too; in the Inishovian worldview their fates were inextricably linked. The fortunes of Inishower had always been experienced through those of the mackerel.

The captain was gripped and moved by the music; before long he succumbed to the urge to bring out his instrument and join in. Some around him stopped playing to listen, but he nodded to them to continue. He quickly picked up the tune, and the eerie tones from the ivory tusks added to the melancholy sense of loneliness and desolation of the piece. The core melody was duly repeated seven times before improvisation around it would begin.

Now the tune was subtly changing; and the change now seemed to come not from the islanders but from the captain's playing. The local musicians dropped into background accompaniment to see where he might be going with it. And it seemed to them that they could hear in the sounds the story of the fish itself: the mackerel in its world, the life in the deep, the changing seasons, the rhythms of migration; the going away and the returning for generation after generation, the knowledge held in the collective cellular memory, in the bones and in the fins. Now the pace of the music was changing again; there were in it flashes of movement, of hunting and being hunted; the swinging darting movement of the shoal, the parting at the predator's swoop, to rejoin once more. There was excitement and exhilaration. The tune was no longer a lament; it had become a celebration.

And then the captain saw that people were up at the front, dancing. The music was growing; the captain's pipes put out a volume and intensity that you wouldn't have credited them for; they could make music that travelled out over a great expanse. And a background rhythmic swell grew up behind the captain's playing from the chorus of other musicians, all of it gathering pace. All sorts were up for the dancing - chubby girls and spotted young males, middle-aged bruisers with bog-stout bellies, lively hags and lean old men. They all moved with lubricity, stepping high with their legs and knees going like mad while the top half of the body remained immobile, in a staid serene world of its own. They had flexibility in the joints from the oil that they got in the fish, the fluid greased energy of the mackerel itself. There were scores dancing in the middle of the bar; now in a tight pack that flitted this way and that across the floor, now deftly moving past one another in zig-zag patterns that rippled and dazzled and flashed. Then the captain realised what was happening: it was the mackerel dance.

Faster and faster they moved, to the accompaniment of a crescendo of stamping and clapping and whooping from the rest of the audience. And then suddenly the dancers just stopped as one. Instantaneously the musicians ceased playing, and so the captain stopped too. There was a long moment of stillness, a unanimous meditation that harked back to the mood of the lament. And then it was straight back to the drinking and talking and arguing and shouting again, as if nothing had happened. That was the way of these things, apparently.

From across the bar the doctor watched Captain Flaherty place his instrument on the table in front of him; he had the look of someone in his element, a man in the right place at the right time, doing the right stuff with the right people. Then the doctor noticed Sally-Anne Peachley move towards the captain. Her body language spoke loudly of seduction and physical intent. The doctor worked his way a bit closer to hear what might be said. Sally-Anne sat herself down to the right of the captain, bubbly and excited; the doctor recognised somewhat proprietorially that squirm of the bottom. She was telling the captain how excited she was about his music. Then she moved closer to him and spoke in a throaty drawl.

"Can I touch your organ?" she said, leaning across him towards the instrument with her left arm so that her right breast pressed against his chest. And there was no mistaking the way she fingered the longest convoluted pipe.

"Oh," she said with a little gasp, "it's much harder than I thought...." And then:

"Do you think I might have a go on it some time?"

The Mackerel

The Atlantic mackerel, Scomber Scombrus, *has held a central place in Inishower's culture since the earliest of times. A migratory pelagic fish, it is well known for its streamlined, tapering form and colouring of ocean blue and silver with distinctive undulating black lines; and it is highly prized for its rich, oily flesh.*

The people of Inishower have realised that there is much more to the mackerel than this. Indeed, Inishovians recognise no less than seventy-five different sub-species, many of which are only found in the deep, nutrient-rich waters off the island's shores. Notable among these are the horse mackerel, the largest variant; the dog mackerel, known for its peculiar habit of following a particular fishing boat wherever it goes; and the cat mackerel, which has small vestigial whiskers around the mouth. Perhaps most interesting to the marine biologist, however, is the relatively large number of subtle hybrids which resemble Scomber Scombrus *but are not true mackerel at all. Most important of these are the false mackerel (Scomber Scurrilus), the sham mackerel (S. Shamulis), the fool's mackerel (S. Duplicitus) and the mock mackerel or mockerel (S. Spuriosis). There is, too, a rare aberration known as the rude mackerel (S. Vulgaris), the only fish known to posses external genitalia.*

Inishovians, then, take their mackerel very seriously. Indeed, the bitter and protracted Mackerel Wars (1690 onwards), assumed by outsiders to have been instigated by disputes about fishing rights, were in fact concerned with arguments over correct identification of these subspecies and varieties.

This family of fishes has appealed to the people in Inishower, for reasons physical or metaphysical, since the dawn of the human era. The ancient festival of Yaoestre or Mackerel Moon, when mackerel of many species shoal locally by night in huge numbers, has been celebrated for at least five thousand years and continues to be observed in today's calendar as St. Scombrel's day. Falling in August, it is the second full moon before the first cross-quarter day after the summer solstice, and marks the zenith of hormonal stimulus in the fishes' annual reproductive cycle.

With scant alternatives for food production on the island owing to extreme climatic circumstances, the mackerel has long represented the staple diet for Inishovians. In the summer season the fish are eaten fresh, but many creative means of preservation have been developed over the millennia to provide stocks for winter and to get them through times of scarcity. The fish are variously dried, smoked, pickled, soused, salted, potted and otherwise cured, incorporating the culinary and preservative properties of a wide variety of the island's native plants.

But of course the mackerel has always provided much more than food. Indeed, it is a reflection of the sacred place occupied by the fish in the islander's cosmology that every part of it has a traditional use and that nothing at all is wasted - from deployment of the sharp gill bones as nibs, to use of the tough, smooth scale-less skin as a prophylactic. On this latter point, some anthropologists believe that many thousands of years of this usage may provide an explanation for the peculiarly tapered physiognomy of the male Inishovian member.[2]

U.o'T.

---

[2] 'The Inishower Prong'

18 Rebel with Menopause

Dr. O'Toole hadn't been able to tell what the enigmatic captain made of Sally-Anne's suggestive advances, or even whether he fully appreciated their bodily content; he seemed to take it as innocent musical enthusiasm, though Niamh at the kitchen door clearly did not. Either way, it was time for the doctor to introduce the evening events. Tonight's top-billed literary celebrity, he announced, had been a legendary figure in the academic world of literature throughout the last half century; he was the godfather of modern literary criticism, Professor Verdigris Levi-Strauss.

Professor Verdigris, now in his nineties, tottered to the front with the aid of an ancient wooden walking frame. He looked weak and frail, but his provincial French voice seemed surprisingly strong and his spirit was clearly irrepressible. A shock of pure white hair exploded from his head in Einsteinian splendour, and he sported a long tufty beard and piercing blue eyes. He wore a thick heavy chocolate-coloured tweed suit with matching waist-coat, and in the pocket carried a heavy gold watch which he insisted on pulling out to consult frequently with the air of a busy man with another pressing engagement straight after this one. Prof. Verdigris regaled the audience with a panoply of literary reminisces and anecdotes, dishing the dirt on prominent figures in the international field of letters and academic criticism - most of whom could do nothing about it as he had already long outlived them. Prof. Verdigris, a lecturing academic through and through, clearly did not care whether his audience were interested in what he had to say, or indeed whether they were listening.

Then Prof. Verdigris backtracked in time and related, in droll scholastic style, the story of his own inception. His mother had been on skiing holiday in the French Alps with her dull and sexually inactive husband Claus Strauss, the son of the Austrian composer Johann Strauss the younger. The erotically disappointed wife met and began a passionate affair with Aaron Levi, then on his way to becoming the first of the great American denim legwear manufacturing magnates, who was here on holiday with his own wife who suffered from chronic vaginismus. The only opportunities the enamoured couple had to meet were snatched moments on remote downhill slopes where they would engage in fumbling, fully clothed acts of improvised intercourse, both with their skis on. It was during one of these frenzied episodes that birth control measures broke down, in an unfortunate and painful incident of prematurity caused by malfunctioning of the prototype Levi trouser zipper, still at an early stage in its development. The couple soon divorced their respective partners, got married, and brought Verdigris Levi-Strauss into the world.

Prof. Verdigris now jumped forwards in time, telling a great many more stories that lacked compellingness to varying degrees; but still he didn't bother whether the audience was interested. He told how he had begun his literary career in social anthropology and moved across into mythology, and then structural linguistics. By this stage, background chat was building up among the audience; people were getting up to go for another round while they still had the previous two on the table. Eyes were glazing over; then heads were lolling and jolting in the time-honoured ritual of pretending not to be asleep. Only the small band of adoring and self-referencing latterday deconstructionists continued to hang on the professor's words.

The professor continued to ramble over his academic exploits of the last half century. By the time he made the startling revelation that he had made up all those absurd ideas about the importance of kinship, ritual and myth and the prevalence of form over content as a kind of studentish joke, nobody much cared.

"Malheuresement," he told the underwhelmed audience, "everyone in ze academic realm took zese concepts completely seriousment, and invented zeories zat proved my ideas right." The whole thing, he said, ended up exerting an absurd degree of influence on literary criticism, on the development of the novel, on cinema and modern lifestyle, and on things people said to one another in order to get laid...

"Quelle bolleux, as you would say in these islands!" rejoiced the Professor. And so he had decided to reveal the whole debacle in his cryptically autobiographical novel, *Portrait de l'Artiste comme Jeune Masterbateur*. But still nobody got it; the work was acclaimed as a masterpiece of postmodernism and taken to prove the validity of the very ideas that he had sought to parody. 'A truly seminal work' it was called, without any hint of irony. And in Squigley's bar too the irony escaped most of the now comatose audience, including the handful of young postmodern *masterbateurs* who were too busy deconstructing what M. Levi-Strauss was saying to properly take it in. Nobody batted an eyelid. What happened next did, however, succeed in batting every eyelid in the place; it was a dull, distant thud that made itself heard and felt throughout the building. An immediate hush fell over the gathering.

"Mon Dieu!" cried Professor Levi-Strauss. "Was zat a beumb?"

It was indeed a *beumb*. In the wake of the sound, the usual visitors went into shock. The usual locals launched into excited gossip-and-conjecture mode. And the usual handful of curious individuals dashed outside to see for themselves what had happened.

What they found was that a historic event was taking place. A distinctive and entirely unprecedented type of rain was falling all over the southern side of the island. It was thick, smoky and deep red in colour, and it was interspersed with many fillets of preserved and flambéed mackerel.

But in the back bar, of course, the chemical generation knew nothing at all about it.

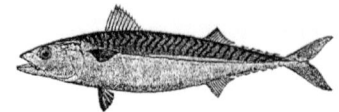

19 A Pagan Plaice

That night Dr. O'Toole slept less but dreamt more than the night before. He lay for hours tossing and turning and trying to escape into unconsciousness, feverishly wondering who had it in for him and why, and what they were going to do next. When he began to doze the doctor found himself standing in a great open Arctic landscape, near the edge of the land; before him was the open sea studded with icebergs, while the snow-covered land behind rose up steeply into a range of jagged icy mountains. The doctor felt frozen to the core, unable to move from where he stood.

Then out to sea, among the platforms of floating ice, the doctor saw that there was a large open boat so crammed full of people that its gunwales were almost at water level. A rope trailed from the boat, and he could see that it had been cut from a mooring on the land; meanwhile, a dark figure starkly outlined against the whiteness was visible fleeing away into the mountains behind. Amongst the occupants of the boat the doctor recognised just about everyone he had ever met on Inishower. They were calling out for him to help them, but the doctor was paralysed. He heard them wish they'd never come to this God-forsaken spot in the first place, and assure him that they certainly wouldn't be back again in a hurry.

Now the doctor noticed the figure of Captain Flaherty sitting atop a distant iceberg, playing his musical instrument. He was clad in his usual nondescript seaman's garb, but didn't seem to feel the cold. Black seals and long-tusked walruses popped their heads out of the water nearby to listen to the music, and then pulled themselves up to sit around him on the ice. Dr. O'Toole tried to call out to the captain, but his words would not carry.

The open boat was now drifting towards the horizon, its occupants still waving for help. On his iceberg the captain was joined by a flock of inquisitive penguins, a pair of arctic foxes and a large polar bear, with other creatures approaching in the water. The ice platform was almost covered in animals of one sort or another, in serene co-existence. The doctor still could not move. Finally, another figure entered the vista: a fair-skinned, bald-pated man clad only in rough brown robes and simple sandals, rowing vigorously across the middle distance in a tiny boat. As he passed by opposite the doctor, he hurled in his direction a stream of foul and abusive cursing.

The doctor drifted into another long bout of troubled semi-wakefulness, in which things that could go wrong with the festival reached increasingly gargantuan proportions in his mind. Then suddenly it was morning. Outside, a thunderous rain driven by a mad wind lashed the windows, seeming fit to burst them. The doctor had long observed that on Inishower the weather conditions closely corresponded with the nature of current events too often to be a coincidence, as if the two phenomena were in some kind of sympathetic relationship. What he'd always wondered was whether island events drew out a corresponding pattern of weather, or if it was quite the other way round.

Either way, Dr. O'Toole did not feel the best. He got up, for he had no choice. Apart from having his own responsibilities to think about, it was St. Scombrel's Day: the biggest day of the year for the community, with special guests laid on, and the Yaoestre ceremony too; and now the mackerel works had been blown up. But life had to go on.

The doctor made it downstairs and into the kitchen, where Niamh was already sitting; you could cut the air with a knife. The doctor stayed quiet, putting on the kettle for a cup of bog-nettle tea; he certainly wasn't going to bring up the subject of the night's damage. Niamh was knitting, and the Cleft of Inishower was on nine and seven eighths; the doctor could not recall a higher reading in his daughter, although he'd known her mother to go completely off the scale once in a while. Niamh was knitting fast and furiously; whatever she was making was having a lot of creative spite put into it. Indeed, a great part of the garment was now in place, arms and body and collar and the rest all in one piece, as was the custom on Inishower. There was none of your pansy knitting of separate pieces and sewing them all together afterwards, like the wimpy *graighaeoil* knitters on the mainland; that sort of bollix wouldn't keep the Inishower weather out for a minute, the island knitting sorority well knew. Towards the end of the job such a garment would tend to become somewhat unwieldy, but that gave the knitters powerful forearms that came in handy for other physical pursuits, not least the wielding of the mackerel clout.

The colourways in this particular garment were now evident, and the doctor inspected it with furtive sideways glances. The background hues merged from deep green at the top, through ocean blue into silver at the midline and on to a rich creamy white below; while striking black undulating bars wove this way and that across the whole of the top half. To tell the truth, the effect was rather striking. Molly had never knitted anything quite like this for the doctor, even in their happier days. Nor indeed had any other knitter he could think of. This was certainly not the same beast that she'd been picking up and putting down for Malachy over the last couple of months.

Sitting in the dark corner by the stove, the doctor continued to watch Niamh. This garment, he realised, was taking the form of the classic Inishower *scrivlin,* [3] and of the oldest and most elaborate form. Maybe it wasn't for Malachy at all. Certainly Niamh would have difficulty making a *scrivlin* for him. Quite apart from their emotional conflicts, the whole tradition of Inishower pullover design militated against it; these garments could only be worn by dyed-in-the-wool writers, and writers who didn't mind the rain. Every feature of their complex design had evolved to meet this stringent specification: the full body length, the cunning three hundred and sixty degree hood, the uniquely tight weave and the dousing in mackerel oil; the multiple stormproof pockets for pens and inks, and the system of tiered pouches for manuscripts in different stages of drafts; the hidden nooks and crannies for snacks so that one can

---

[3] Modern derivative of the ancient term 'scriobholainn', literally 'thing of wool for a writer'.

keep writing rather than having access to an excuse to take a break from writing - all these features would be both unnecessary and objectionable to someone like Malachy. For the old-fashioned *scrivlin* is not so much a pullover as a writer's support system. The unique shoulder design with its deliberate limitation of movement and prevention of raising the arms, evolved over the aeons to keep writers at their work, would not be welcomed by him either. So if it wasn't for Malachy, who was if for? And was Niamh turning against Malachy at last? There couldn't be any harm in that, the doctor thought. He wouldn't put it past her to be unforgiving at this point; non-delivery of mackerel without an explanation would be enough in itself.

The doctor had never seen his daughter knit with such sheer energy. And now it looked like she was running out of wool. She'd have to go up soon to the knitting collective's store and dyeworks on the hillside to get more. That was good, he thought. It would be ideal if she was out of the way for his surgery sessions this morning, in case any juicy cases turned up.

As it turned out there weren't any juicy cases in the morning surgery session, and the burdensome events of St. Scombrel's eve hung over the doctor as he worked. Instead of succulent sex-related problems there was a steady stream of people with difficulties related to the explosions. The events were now affecting people's writing, and shaking the collect island psyche to its core. All kinds of literary phobias and neuroses were surfacing. Boxty Falloon was finding that he couldn't tolerate any loud noises in his work, which was limiting because of his specialisation in Wild West adventure stories. Bridie Boru couldn't bring herself to write about sudden or unexpected events. Half a dozen different local writers had noticed mysterious and malevolent lurking figures unsolicitedly popping up in their work, which was disastrous for them all because they were variously engaged in the genres of light romance, positive thinking self-help manuals and nursery school texts. A whole clutch of other resident writers had found that the only mode that they could engage in was a sort of terse, suspenseful whodunnit style full of helpless victims, explosive situations and underlying sense of evil. And overlaying all these problems was a pervasive preoccupation with non-availability of mackerel in everyone's work. Even visiting authors were being affected.

Normally such cases wouldn't motivate the doctor as much as this; but things were different now, and after seeing a couple of patients he found that it was taking his mind off his own problems. For the doctor had long and valuable experience of treating writer's ailments; it interested him more than with the dull round of mundane physical problems like shattered limbs or life-threatening illnesses. And he was good at treating literary complaints, empowered by the knowledge he had acquired on the specialised usages of native herbs and other traditional remedies. The plants of the island's perpetually saturated boglands, he believed, had a profound symbiotic relationship with that of the people, both having evolved together in the same unique environmental system. The ancient sages and healers of the island knew that for every human ill there existed a corresponding curative plant out there in the boglands, if only you knew where to find it and how to use it.

Indeed the doctor had for many years gathered some of the most used herbs into his little medicinal water garden at the back of the house: Purple Gloomberry, an excellent remedy for writer's depression; Lesser Mindswell for stimulating the jaded imagination; Scribe's Garlic, which he had often prescribed for literary viruses; Marsh Nipplewort and the aphrodisiac Pronghorn fungus, both long recognised for treating loss of the erotic impulse in writing; and of course St. Scombrel's Ease, a panacea for all mackerel-related complaints - a herb which he was administering today to almost every patient.

Drawing on these resources, the doctor provided tinctures and salves for his visitors this morning. When all had departed he sat at his desk, looking out over the damp landscape towards where the enigmatic bulk of Fishtail Mountain stood. This sort of quick-fix response to people's problems was all very well, he knew; but there was a deeper malaise behind the catastrophes, that needed something more fundamental to deal with. Yet something in that scene told him that he would find the means to deal with it in the very mystical traditions that were buried in this landscape.

In the kitchen the doctor found Niamh and the captain. Niamh had returned from the wool depot and was knitting again; the mysterious garment looked almost finished. The captain sat quietly by the stove, looking into the fire. Nobody was speaking, but the doctor noticed that the cleft was now down to six or so - a remarkable drop, considering the circumstances.

More surprising still was what happened next. Niamh had just finished one of the sleeves on the *scrivlin* when she got up, walked over to the captain and placed it against his arm. It was a little longer than his.

"That'll be fine," she said, still wearing her knitter's glare of concentration, "once you've got a bit of rain on it." And she strode back to her seat. The doctor's jaw fell and the captain's eyes were set wide open. She returned the gaze of each in turn and went straight on with the knitting.

"Well, you'll be needing something better," she said finally, exhibiting no discernible change of expression, "than that bollix you're wearing now." She paused. "When this one's finished we'll take yours out and give it a *doghtering*[4]"

The doctor wondered what was going on. When he thought about it, blowing up the island's mackerel facilities would be just about the worst thing anyone could do, on a par with the most heinous crime against knitting, in Niamh's book. So it looked like she wasn't holding the captain to blame for that. But was it a

---

[4] Literally *doghteiracht*, Inishower's traditional thirteenth century inquisitional ceremony in which an individual was burnt at the stake for adhering to heretical views on knitting.

coincidence that Malachy's garment had simultaneously aborted too?

Either way, the doctor didn't have time to wonder for he had an afternoon masterclass to attend to; so he left them to it. But it was with a noticeably lighter step that he walked out into the sleety torrent now falling out of the sky, skewed at a nasty angle by the stiff wind still blowing out of the west. He also noticed a stupid grin on his own face as he turned it into the wind and rain; and he marched off towards the library.

The Wonder of Wool

The knitting tradition on the island of Inishower is a wondrous thing in itself. This highly specialised craft has been an integral part of the culture since the earliest times. Indeed, the Inishovians have long seen it as a close metaphorical cousin of written storytelling - a form where strands of wool are woven together as are words and ideas, creating the true origins (Inishovian, of course) of the now universal metaphor of "a good yarn".

The Inishovian Dampfaced Merino sheep is descended from a strain of wild goat that is indigenous only to this location; its wool contains more natural fibre strength and moisture-repelling oils than any known animal fibre. Domestication and selective breeding over the millennia have made it the most muttonless variety of sheep known to man, for the creature has put all its resources into producing a weather-resistant coat. Consequently, the damp-faced Merino is inedible. Wandering over the lower reaches of Fishtail Mountain, both sheep and wool have been profoundly affected by the mountain's special environmental influences. The fleece itself has evolved into a unique form, not unlike that of a thatched roof, with a ridge-like feature along the animal's back and a steep pitch on each side to throw off the heaviest torrents of rain. The lowest tips of wool curl back up to form vestigial guttering that directs away the run-off, giving a measure of protection to the legs.

A unique prehistoric form of knitting evolved on the island to avail of this specialised resource, and to produce specialised garments that would work as well for people as for sheep in the challenging micro-climate. Textile anthropologists have termed this most ancient ancestor of knitting methods "Wet Isle", and observed in it a number of technical developments that are found nowhere else. To get a tight knit and minimise moisture penetration in the finished garment, for instance, the fibres are spun thickly, yet the knitting needles have to be extremely fine. The wool is so strong that it can support a man's weight, and some of the needles so slim that they are almost invisible to the naked eye, explaining a traditional taboo against using them near haystacks. To tighten the knit further, the tension is kept high; hence Inishovian knitters can be identified by peculiar knotted muscles like tiny biceps on the index fingers of both hands, and by their deeply furrowed brows and short tempers.

In ancient times, the desirable properties of Inishovian knitwear became known far and wide. On their way to Iceland, Scandinavian Vikings would row thousands of sea miles out of their way to avail themselves of the knitted garments that so well threw off the sea spray which was the bane of their lives in open boats. At the same time they would have to lay waste to the island so as not to show they were just there on a clothing acquisition spree. While pillaging Inishower, however, they took care to kill neither knitters nor sheep, so that the prized supplies would be available on future visits.

The prominent part played by knitting in the island's traditional customs is still very much in evidence; one surviving ritual of initiation is worth particular mention. To this day, the visitor arriving by boat is traditionally accosted by welcoming islanders; while standing with one foot on the quay and the other still in the boat, travellers must subject themselves to the procedure of being measured for a knitted garment. Since this involves up to twenty-six different anatomical dimensions, and because the swell can be heavy, this is a memorable and often painful experience for the unwary arrival.

U.o'T.

20 Death of a Naturist

The masterclass was a mixed bag, to say the least. Most of the students were too affected by the troubles to concentrate on carnal priorities in their work. O'Dowdy and Thinkwell, anxious and preoccupied, were slipping back into their old ways. But Sally-Anne Peachley was going from strength to strength - shining, in fact. The work she handed in today was titled *Penises of Inishower*. Sally-Anne had discovered the phenomenon of the Inishower Prong; indeed she'd made some very acute observations about it. While noting that all native *peni* tapered, she'd observed a significant variation in the degree of narrowing, with one or two extreme cases approaching a conical form. Her dissertation covered not only what these organs looked like but also how they functioned in practice, with extensive comparative data on insertion and withdrawal syndromes, duration statistics and patterns of ejaculation. A concluding section neatly entitled *Coming to a Point* summarised her findings in spreadsheet format. It was a learned yet lively document, much of which was news to the doctor. Even if she hadn't got around to investigating the corresponding adaptations in female Inishower genitalia - a subject which he had explored in some depth in his youth - it was nevertheless it a remarkable body of work.

This case study, Sally-Anne intimated with pride, was based on "extensive field research". That research, the doctor reasoned, must have been compressed into little more than the last twenty-four hours or so. How many cases had she sampled? And she looked so fresh; this truly was a remarkable woman.

Well, the doctor thought, her focus seemed to have shifted away from Captain Flaherty for the moment. Perhaps it was time to issue her an invitation to a private surgery session. But then Niamh would never let her near the house - he could just feel the mackerel clout now. What a shame. So he had to content himself with telling her that he thought the piece very workmanlike; she clearly took this as a compliment. And of course he'd need to take it home for closer study...

That evening Dr. O'Toole and the captain set out for McDadgh's in weather that was easing off into little more than a gentle downpour; they might even see a bit of the full moon later on. The doctor was feeling unsteady, yet not so black as he'd been earlier in the morning. And Niamh had surprised him by saying she hoped the evening went well; apparently she was going to stay at home to finish the *scrivlin*. The captain walked alongside him now with long and loose stride. He'd spent his own day away on a long walk by himself, and judging by the bits and pieces attached to his boots the doctor reckoned he must have walked over most of the island.

There'd certainly be a great night of it at McDadgh's as far as the festival was concerned; it was an evening of poetry, as St. Scombrel was known for his love of fifth century Inishovian haiku; and the main attraction was the island's greatest living poet - a figure whose work was celebrated worldwide, though he himself had never set foot abroad. And then there was the Yaoestre ceremony itself. It would be a big night all right.

McDadgh's was packed to the gills once more; the mood, however, was a mixture of apprehension and discontent. The latest atrocity had indeed struck the community at its heart; it wasn't just that essential food supplies would be running out in a matter of days - the whole thing felt like an attack on the island's spiritual heritage. People wished to see action taken. They wanted the culprit found and handed over to be 'dealt with properly' - a reference to the islanders' traditionally gruesome methods of punishing individuals who offend against any of the 'holy trinity' of mackerel, writing or knitwear. Corbel McLintol, Finbar McFogarty and some of the more practically minded islanders were talking of taking the law into their own hands if nothing was done.

But what could be done, the doctor asked them? They still didn't know who was responsible. People had their suspicions, of course. There was the usual clutch of accusations fuelled by lifelong patterns of rivalry and hatred. Yet the most ardent *vendettistes* were reluctant to believe that even their mortal enemies would go so far as to blow up the mackerel warehouse - especially on St. Scombrel's Eve. So the net was being cast wider, and visitors were not free of suspicion. Some folks were certainly wondering about the mysterious and enigmatic Captain Flaherty; but the doctor pointed out that the man hadn't been out of his sight for a minute during the whole of the day and evening before.

And then of course there was the question of Malachy. Disappearing like this didn't look good. Now that he wasn't supplying the fish, people were beginning to admit how much they disliked him. But they stopped short of serious bad-mouthing, because you never know when you might have to depend upon someone again in the future; the strand of fishing DNA was a rare thing in the Inishower gene pool. There was the usual plethora of alleged sightings of a furtive, tattered figure, including stories of someone in the vicinity of Dr. O'Toole's cottage itself; but the doctor dismissed these as the stuff of creativity and literary inventiveness. He very much doubted that, since Malachy would hardly risk getting within a mile of Niamh if he was still around.

And many of the visitors weren't happy with things either. Yet the more romantic American would-be writers and tourist types savoured the ambience of impending violence and danger; they quite fancied the sense of living at the cutting edge of literary action. Others felt that their own writing would benefit osmotically from soaking up the buzz and adrenaline of it all - not to mention the first-hand experience of explosives, crime and destruction that was more valuable than any amount of research.

But the rest of the visitors were nervous or downright scared. The de Boyle set hadn't ventured out of their rented cottage for the last thirty-six hours. They'd set up a continuous watch round the clock, convinced that it was only a matter of time before they were attacked, blown up, kidnapped or otherwise brutalised. The thought that each day might be their last only added urgency to their tendency to cram as much incestuous coupling into the time that was left. And thoughts of unspeakable sexual acts they might soon be forced to carry out upon one another at gunpoint added further to their highly excitable state.

Other visitors had had enough, and just wanted to go home. And nobody wanted to go home more than the fringe elements of posers and hangers on, the press representatives and party-goers, the literary agents, talent scouts and assorted ne'er-do-wells - the collected ranks of the gutterati. Suddenly, being seen with the right people seemed less important than keeping one's limbs attached to one's body, or one's brains inside one's skull.

These people and others wanted to leave, but they couldn't; there was no boat. So large numbers of them stood around nervously in McDadgh's, seeking safety in numbers, trying to get to the centre of any knot of people so as to be cushioned against any sudden blast from whatever direction it might come. In this way they created an impression of so many tall and unhappy penguins huddling together against the icy blast at the windswept north pole in the middle of winter.

So everybody was wondering what was going to go up next, but nobody mentioned that. Despite the ugly mood this was still Inishower. And on Inishower it took a lot to demolish the native inhabitants' creative instinct and ability to glean positive potential out of the worst situation. Hence the news that active locals clearing up after the explosion this morning had discovered in the fishy fall-out from the blast a brand-new island delicacy. The mackerel dilettantes' talk was of a full-bodied, smoky flavour tinged with complex and interesting notes of nitro-glycerine and dynamite. It might not catch on as a regular food item, but there was enough to serve as a very handy bar snack and this helped to cheer things up ahead of tonight's entertainments. So the dark piscine cloud hanging over Inishower had a somewhat silver lining.

When the bar snacks had run out, the doctor decided to get things going. He rounded up the slim poets clutching their volumes of self-penned verse; they were out in force tonight as the introductory act for the Greatest Living Poet. Most would later make mileage out of being on the same bill as the great man..."Yah, of course I've gigged a great deal with the GLP, he likes to have me do his warm-up for him, usually asks for me. I always look him up whenever I'm on Inishower..."

Ready to go on, the slim poets clustered together now in varying degrees of nervous excitement, probably the only people in the building not thinking somewhere in their brain about explosions. All were in the *de rigeur* colour coding of black clothing with black accessories and black make-up; all were pale and wan of skin; altogether they gave a convincing impression of people who should get out more. None were locals - island poets constituted another breed altogether; for a start, they had a modicum of skin colour, and some flesh on their bones.

As the performances got under way, a pattern emerged. Each slim poet would shuffle to the front with his or her slight works and deliver a couple of pieces of varying length but equal intensity. There would be a deeply tortured element in the overall manner, implying some deep personal tragedy that verified the profundity and gravity of their work. Subject matter too was covered by such cultural agreements; despair and desolation were popular, together with the twin torments of not wanting to be like other people and at the same time feeling rejected for being different. The accepted mode of delivery was a monotonous whine, punctuated by sudden emphasis on random words or phrases.

It was difficult, therefore, for the audience to distinguish between these various performers, who no doubt each saw themselves as a true individual and a genius to boot; though the crowd could tell that certain individuals were undeniably female and certain others were probably male. Yet one or two candidates managed to pick themselves out. A relatively blithe spirit by the name of Moonbeam Strobelite excelled herself with the sheer extremity of her depressed self-obsession, in a poem entitled *Me Me Me Me Me*. Byron Shelley Gimlett's work seemed to be about anger at his parents' forcing him to become a poet by giving him that particular name. The feminist poet Dildo McCann was briefly memorable for the incandescent wrath that she poured over previous lovers. If there'd been a prize for plumbing the depths of melancholic gloom and abject despair it could not have been denied to Caspar Grindley for his elegiac piece, *I Always Knew This World Was Not the Place for Me*, accompanied on guitar in the country and western style. These offerings left listeners querying just how much world-weariness and knowledge of the profound uselessness of existence could legitimately have been acquired by people who were little over nineteen.

The audience also had trouble with a disturbing piece by Felicity Sprite on the joys of self-mutilation, and an equally unwelcome effort by Jonathan Boyle on his innovative solo sexual practices. Both of these were thankfully short; not so Sylvia Dyke's epic poem about skirting boards, which the doctor felt obliged to interrupt at the forty-seventh stanza; the audience, respectful as ever in the Inishovian tradition, was visibly relieved. Perhaps, the doctor suggested, they could all hear more of Ms. Dyke's versification next year, or possibly the one after that. A break now seemed in order.

During the interval the doctor was approached by a vast and daunting American poet in a vivid Hawaiian shirt and matching shorts, who introduced himself as Rameses Z. Schwartzenburger. Rameses clearly viewed himself as God's gift to the world of poetry, and was clear that he was going to do a spot in the second half. That wasn't how things worked in the festival, the doctor tried to explain to him, but this fell into the category of things that Rameses didn't want to hear; and he did not seem to be a man that was used to taking no for an answer. The doctor, over-awed by his sheer physical bulk, said he would 'see what he could do'; and Rameses rolled back to his seat, taking up most of the front row. The doctor forgot all about it, and went for a quick whizz round McDadgh's to see what gossip he could catch up on. There wasn't much of that about; only the rumour that a bunch of locals led by Corbel McLintol were doing a bit of vigilante work, keeping an eye on things round the village. So far they had nothing to report. That was reassuring.

Now the doctor reckoned it was time to get going with the big event. He was personally excited about it; he liked the Greatest Living Poet - everybody did. But when the doctor announced, "Ladies and gentlemen, please welcome the greatest poet of our time...", he was horrified to see the immense form of Rameses Z. Schwartzenburger launch itself towards the front. As the applause faltered, the doctor had to intercept the bulky presence and explain that he was actually introducing someone else. Rameses did not like this. So the doctor whispered to him that he was to be top of tonight's bill, preceded by the local poet. Rameses seemed happy with this, and returned to his seat like a tidal backwash. Now Hamish Shooney came to the front from the back of the bar, where he'd been waiting in his usual unprepossessing manner.

Hamish Shooney's presence was imposing only in the quietest of ways; the man emanated warmth from his ruddy cheeks and eyes that seemed to be permanently closed in perpetual laughter. His modesty was legendary; he was a simple farmer-poet, spending his life writing poems about the earth and digging and matters of the land, as a commentary on the process of life itself. And yet he was revered not only on Inishower but in the outside world too. His collections were best-sellers from Afghanistan to Zimbabwe; he edited anthologies and translated classics from other cultures; he'd been awarded the Nobel prize for poetry about vegetables. But he was unspoiled by all of this; he chose to stay on in Inishower, living a quiet life on his ancestral farm on the lower slopes of the mountain, keeping a few merinos and sending his bit of wool to the collective, though he certainly didn't need the money these days. And not a soul begrudged him this success, not even on Inishower. He was the only person on the island that nobody could think of a reason to start a vendetta with. And he encouraged other island poets; he was generous with tips and contacts, and would exert a bit of influence in the publishing world on somebody else's behalf. He was a rare thing altogether, and everybody knew it.

As Shooney read from his work, you could hear an Inishower needle drop. His voice was earthy and mellifluous, full of small potatoes and the honest toil of digging. His verses spoke of the hoe and the rake and the beloved spade; of their feel in the hand, the reality of hard graft and manual effort; of work in the fields, the digging of turf and the long journey home. They spoke of childhood and family and the forefathers that had gone before - the generations of writers and poets and diggers on the small farm. They evoked the ancestral spirits that lay beneath the surface of the daily round. They catalogued the ancient leathery bodies found while cutting the turf, preserved and mummified by the bog water, accompanied by flagons of archaic whiskey and medieval casks of butter that you could still eat today. They stirred into life the dormant strands of ancient consciousness that still lurked within the mind of modern man on Inishower - the neolithic strains in the psyche, the stone-age instincts lurking in the bones and blood. They pondered the habit of primitive conflict between generation after generation of the island's warring factions - son after father, daughter after mother - in self-perpetuating cycles of vengeance and retribution.

But Shooney's verses offered too a physical celebration of the fecundity of nature and the natural realm: the gathering of the wild harvests from hedge and spinney; the rhythmic reassuring cycles of the seasons by which a man marked off his allotted span, and measured his progress. They embraced the archetypal elements of the landscape on which the Inishovian's life is played out - the rich brown Flushey river winding to the sea, the lush purple bogland slowly releasing its secrets, the grey overarching bifurcated presence of the big mountain.

And in no way separately from any of this, Shooney illuminated the nature of the writer's and the poet's art itself; for to him the tilling of the fields was one with the crafting of the poem's furrowed landscape, the hewing of meaningful experiences from the rough earth of life's raw matter. His poems spoke to the islanders and to the world in a language they could understand: the language of real work and real stuff and the sharp, hard textures of common objects, sifting from these the realisation of eternal truths. The poems celebrated the extraordinariness of the everyday, and the down-to-earthness of the transcendent. And finally they admitted the eternal quandary of the poet and the writer who, in the last analysis, is guilty of dealing in mere words rather than real actions.

The poems were physical, tangible realities; the listeners received them with the sense of touch as much as of hearing or vision. The consonants tumbled together in a rich clatter, leaving an indelible imprint on the topography of the senses. The audience moved with him, local and visitor alike, through the lyrical, haunting web of time and place that he wove. It was a million miles from the self-absorbed verbal fumblings of the black-clad youngsters that had never wielded a fork or cut hay. He was the writer's writer and the poet's poet. And when he finished, the solid content of his last poem reverberated round the room in a long, absorbed silence:

DEATH OF A NATURIST

The never-ending summer of our youth
Was thick with fecund nuts and crunchy roots;
Daily we'd garner berries, cram our guts
And faces, with fermenting fleshy fruits.

Or gather at the green-pond's fetid edge
To jellied-eyeball toadspawn freely take;
Pull turgid eels from every slimy nook,
Drag dark-striped pike from out the sloe-black lake.

We followed in our father's plough-worn path,
And learned hard lessons from his belt and cuff.
We mastered crafts of raking up plump spuds -
The roughish cut and thrust of turf and stuff.

Or else we'd dig for rotting bones and skulls,
Shrouded from ancient times in mist and fog;
Poke at the shattered ribs of murdered Celts,
Or pull full-festering corpses from the bog.

Then, in the midst of summer's sultry bake,
Where river's sinewy outline twists and curls,
We'd dive into its chilly waters, nude;
Then show our shrivelled willies to the girls.

My digging now is for the poem's truths,
My hunt no longer for primeval turds;
My gathering of fruits the verbal kinds;
All I flash, now, is metaphors and words.

For recognition's hit me with brash clout;
Now all I do is look, and sit, and write;
Gone are the days of grime and dirty work -
I am a bloody lucky oul' gob-shite[1].
- Hamish Shooney

---

[1] See note at back of book

21 De Altitudinis

Mr. Shooney thoughtfully finished his reading at five minutes to midnight, leaving just enough time for the Yaoestre day ritual of which he was to be this year's honorary beneficiary. The crowd gathered tightly round to witness this most sacred of Inishower events, administered by Dr. O'Toole. It was the symbolic healing of St. Scombrel, the laying on of the mackerel - the greatest honour that Inishower could bestow upon one of its own. On this occasion the blessing had to be executed with a charred fragment rescued from yesterday's disaster. Yet this in no way diminished the sanctity of the occasion; indeed it was a confirmation of the islanders' robust phlegmatism, their enthusiastic improvisational spirit and keen sense of irony, that the occasion was enhanced by this usage of a truly burnt offering. It's what St. Scombrel would have wanted, the locals agreed.

And now the great day had safely come to an end. An air of palpable relief that there had been no further mishap steadily gave way to unbridled celebration. There was drinking and partying and riotous excess in the true spirit of Inishower for most of the night, though the doctor went home early to a well-earned sleep. Rameses got to do his gig, with a literally captive audience consisting of the entire group of slim poets, looking all the paler and wanner and thinner and more desolate than ever after three and a half hours of non-stop exposure to Rameses' material. Hopefully they learned something from the experience.

Right in the middle of the night, though, the unwanted happened - even if barely audible this time. It was the softest, gentlest, fluffiest kind of thud that anyone had every heard; most people took some persuading that it was an explosion at all. But those who dashed outside were assured by what they saw that something had indeed gone up in smoke. For in the damp blurred moonlight they were greeted by the falling of the second radically new kind of Inishower precipitation in as many days. This time it was a misty drizzle enriched by a panoply of multi-coloured strands of wool that now drifted down from the sky on the soft westward wind, like some sort of psychedelic tickertape. It was something that the chemical generation in the back room would have really appreciated, if only they'd known that anything had happened; but they didn't.

22 The Call of The Mild

Dr. O'Toole awoke refreshed from a deep and peaceful sleep. He felt good; yesterday had been a resounding success. He rose and walked to the window, where the glass was covered with a precipitation too fine to deserve the title of rain. He looked out, and blinked. Rubbing his eyes, he looked again. The landscape before him appeared to have been decorated in the night with profuse coloured woolly tendrils, lying all over his garden and beyond. The sky was bright, and minute refracting droplets of moisture adhered to the fluffy filaments causing them to glitter like some kind of rainbow frosting. Something was not quite right.

Two minutes later, wearing his wool tweeds and boots, the doctor stepped out of the house. The flossy array of filigree strands lay everywhere - on the road, over the fields, across bushes and trees and even over the roof of the house. By the time he'd examined a piece of the disintegrated fibre at close quarters he knew what had happened. He set off right away down to the village with no thought of breakfast.

Just before the doctor reached there, however, he detected an odour that spoke loudly to his stomach and took his mind back more decades than he cared to remember: a delicious mixture of wood smoke and mackerel fat and blackening crispy fish-skin. He saw a plume of pale blue smoke over by the south-eastern shore; as he walked towards it the smell grew stronger.

At the source of the smoke, Captain Flaherty sat on the beach by a small fire made from driftwood. Beside him was his boxed instrument, and at the edge of the water a good pile of mackerel; they glistened with the vibrant hues only possessed when just out of the water. Two of the largest were roasting on hazel spits over the fire; the oil dripping from them fed the flames, causing them to spill their inflammable juices all the more. Wool related disasters were set aside for the moment.

The captain heard Dr. O'Toole approach across the shingle.

"Good morning, doctor," he said. "Will you have a fish for breakfast?"

"I will," replied the doctor. The captain waved him over to sit on the battered box. The two men ate the fish with their fingers in a silence that wasn't much short of religious. The doctor recalled the times when his father had brought him down as a boy to the shore each year with the first mackerel of the season, and they'd cook them over a fire just like this, right down to the hazel skewers; and then they'd say a prayer to St. Scombrel and eat the fish in this perfect assembly of smell, taste, drizzle and fresh air. Then they'd return with the rest of the first fish to a clout around the ear for each of them from Ulick's mother, for not bringing them up to her earlier.

When the two men had finished eating they sat on in silence. The doctor's mind could now be applied again to the awful thing that had happened in the night, and what on earth he was going to do about it; but he did not speak of these things. The captain sat on with his back to the sea, looking fixedly towards the shape of the Fishtail Mountain; and the two of them stayed that way for a time - the doctor observing the captain, and the captain observing the mountain.

When the two arrived home, the cleft of Inishower was at a paralysing 9.7 and Niamh's pale face had gone black with rage. Next thing there was a rabble of voices outside the house, and a pounding at the front door. The doctor opened it to find the assembled representative knitters of Inishower with a nasty collection of furrowed brows amongst them. They were here to deliver an ultimatum, they said; Mabel McLintol was the spokeswoman, well-known as having the worst temper of the lot. The gist of it was that they were ordering their writing menfolk to get off their arses and search the island for the perpetrator of this latest and most heinous of all atrocities, and bring him back to face the music which would certainly be no lullaby. And there'd be no drinks beforehand this time for the menfolk to steady their nerves or any of that bollix. This wasn't something they were asking the doctor, by the way; they were telling him.

Mrs. McLintol looked at Niamh, and Niamh didn't argue. Then the deputation turned on their collective heel and marched back down to the village, probably looking a good deal more fearsome than any assembly their husbands were likely to be able to put together.

The male posse was being shepherded together outside Mickey Squigley's; Mabel McLintol and a bunch of the knittingfolk guarded the doors of the pub to make sure that none of them darted in for a so-called 'swift one', while a splinter group carried out similar duties at McDadgh's.

Under pressure from his wife, Corbel McLintol did his best to pull the crowd together, and Finbar McFogarty lent a hand too, but the men were clearly not there of their own volition. They'd been decked out in whatever weaponry and protective equipment came to hand. Cormac Flannelly had brought a hay fork; Bran Moughan had a rolling pin and some sharp pastry cutters. Boxty Falloon brought along only a couple of pens. Bouncer McCall possessed nothing but his considerable bulk. Minty McGinty probably had the most useful accoutrements in the form of a long and pointy sheep crook and a bad-tempered merino ram that was pawing the ground and straining on the bit of string Minty had him on. Most of the men had thick wads of manuscript inside their clothing as precaution against possible attack; in the case of Joe Quillory and Seumas Reame, though, it was as much to protect themselves from one another with extra thickness provided to the back. These non-volunteers were joined by Dezzy Boru and Patsy McBride - the only two male knitters on the island, and not very good at their job either as they only did it because their wives were writers. These two were clad in the densest grade knitwear, originally developed in the Anglo-Norman era for protection against arrows.

By now a bunch of visitors had come out of Squigley's to see what was going on. Sir Lancelot and Bryony de Boyle were grinning and pointing; maybe they'd twigged that whoever had it in for someone wasn't after them, and they'd be okay so long as they stayed away from anything to do with literature, mackerel or wool. Then Mickey Squigley came out of the bar and suggested that a blessing be given to the posse by his good self; and while all knitters' eyes were closed in fervent prayer, he managed to slip a quarter bottle of Bogeen brand whiskey into the pocket of each communicant.

"And if any one of our loved ones here gathered should not come back," he said in unctional tones, "then at least he will have died happy" - here a couple of knitterish eyes opened in suspicion, and Mickey quickly added - "...to have given his life for his community in this noble, selfless and eminently worthwhile endeavour." He seemed to get away with it; and so the crew set off for the back of the island.

At the doctor's masterclass that afternoon Sally-Anne Peachley continued to rival her own previous records of sexual curiosity. Today's work took the form of imaginative autobiography; it was an extended piece that centred quite explicitly on the penis of Captain Flaherty and elaborated on all the things that she would like to do with it. On presenting the essay she enquired of the doctor whether she might perhaps accompany him home and pay a visit to the subject of her speculative work, purely in the interests of academic verification. The doctor did not think it a good idea, even without taking into account what Niamh would have to say on the subject. In that case, Sally-Anne asked, could the doctor kindly ask Captain Flaherty to run his eye over the piece, and possibly give her feedback on a later occasion? It was possible, the doctor replied, pocketing the document - purely in the interests of his own vicarious pursuits later on. He left the library straight away with the sheaf of papers in his hand.

The doctor returned home to find Niamh in a somewhat improved state. Her facial mode had gone from black to mid grey, and the cleft was ranging between seven and eight, which could still be dangerous depending on whether rising or dropping. The smell of fresh cooked mackerel filled the kitchen; that would have helped. Two plates with a pair of skeletons on each were on the table. Captain Flaherty's music came through the open door to the hallway. Niamh was knitting, putting the finishing touches to the *scrivlin*.

"What do you think of it?" she asked him, holding up the garment in its bold hues of green-blue and silver, and black bars.

"It's a fine thing all right," replied the doctor. "Your mother would be proud of making such a garment." He eyed the cleft; it was definitely on the way down.

"The posse's off to find Malachy," risked the doctor. "They're going to search the whole island." He paused. Niamh had gone a bit blacker, but said nothing; she just clenched her teeth and returned to crafting the complex guttered bottom hem.

"I think I'd best be off to the surgery," said the doctor quickly. "I've some patients coming in." Niamh could tell he was lying, but was happy for him to be out of her sight.

"Send Captain Flaherty in," she said. "I need to do a preliminary fitting." Now the cleft was dropping again. The doctor couldn't remember it so changeable.

When the captain left the surgery, the doctor settled down at his desk. He was glad to have no patients; he needed to do some serious thinking. In fact his whole presentation of the history of Inishower was going to need review, in the light of recent events. Had there been precedents for this kind of thing, for instance? Did the past hold clues to a solution that he'd overlooked? He might have missed out on something important. He was going to have to go back to the beginning and study it afresh.

But before he embarked on that lengthy process, he yielded to a baser urge to have a quick look through Sally-Anne's new piece of work. It was the least he could do - his duty as a tutor. He reached into his pocket for the sheaf of notes; they weren't there. They weren't on his desk either. And they weren't in the drawer where he usually put sensitive material awaiting perusal. He tried to think. He definitely had them in his hand when he came home...

A heavy stinging blow caught his right ear and wrenched his skull round through ninety degrees. His head reeled; a small galaxy passed before his eyes. His stomach churned and threatened to reject its contents. He put his hand to his ear, while a tape recorder inside his brain played back the swishing sound that had been eclipsed by the surge of pain. How intimately he knew that combination of sight, sound and touch, bestowed over the decades by three generations of O'Toole women. Niamh stood behind him, shaking Sally-Anne's pages. Her face was now purple.

"Call yourself a tutor? This isn't literary work, it's filth and rubbish. When I get my hands on the whore that wrote this I'll give her something she won't dislodge in a hurry." Niamh strode out of the surgery and nearly took the door off its hinges slamming it behind her. The doctor turned back to his desk; his vision was still blurred; his temple throbbed. Maybe things were better when there weren't fresh mackerel about.

After a considerable time he was able to focus on the prescription pad in front of him; and he began to write:

The history of the island of Inishower is an endless story of invasions, disillusionment, literary conundrums, and excessive moisture...

Presently the surgery door burst open and the bulky form of Corbel McLintol stumbled into the room. Blood seeped from a terrible wound in his groin; the smell of bog whiskey came in with him as well. The doctor looked up from his reverie of writing. It was what he had feared. Thoughts flew through his mind: is this what things are coming to? Is this the destiny of our island? Nevertheless he responded with restraint.

"So you've been in the wars, Corbel," he said. "Somebody's taking things too far this time." He opened a drawer in his desk, filled an anaesthetic syringe and approached his patient.

"Ah, sure 'tis nothing to worry about," replied the big man, brushing aside the proffered anaesthetic needle. He scarcely winced as the doctor dressed the wound. Then Corbel's nose twitched.

"Is that fresh mackerel I can smell?"

"Don't ask," said the doctor; and Corbel didn't.

"And where did you manage to obtain this structural alteration to your anatomy?" asked the doctor as he worked.

"We found Malachy," replied McLintol, "when we went up to his house. He legged it when he saw us coming, and we chased after him. But we'd drink taken and we couldn't catch him. He ran up the mountain..." Corbel winced as the doctor pulled the stitching tight.

"Yes?"

"When he got to the mountain none of the others would go after him, only me. I started up the path, but he started rolling rocks down. One of them hit me, and I thought I'd better come back."

"It's a good thing you did," said the doctor. "I'd say you've lost a bit of blood there. You'd better have a couple of pints of stout."

"I'd best be off then. I've got to break the news to Mabel that we didn't get Malachy. And he's the trouble-maker all right."

"What makes you so sure of that?"

"We found this book in his house when we came back down." He searched with his big hands in the capacious pockets of his jacket.

"A book at Malachy's house?" said the doctor. "Malachy never read a word in his life. What would he be doing with a book?"

"Here it is," said Corbel, pulling out a dog-eared square paperback volume and handing it over. The doctor flicked through it; the book was all pictures. Several sections were particularly well-thumbed and grimy. It was entitled *Terrorism for Beginners - an illustrated guide.*

When the doctor had finished, Corbel donned his heavy tweed trousers and jacket and shambled out; he didn't need to put his cap back on, for he had never taken it off. On Inishower you only did that in the most extreme circumstances.

TERRORISM FOR BEGINNERS

- an illustrated guide

Big Bang Press

CONTENTS

Equipment you will need

How to get started

Never tell anyone what you're doing

Choosing targets

How to avoid getting caught

Urban terrorism

Rural terrorism

How to blow things up

How to kill people

How to not get caught*

How to construct a small thermo-nuclear device

* don't skip this chapter

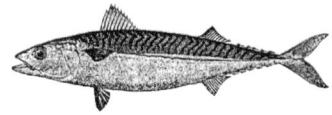

23 Ring of Dark Water

Doctor O'Toole, slumped in his chair, awoke with a start. Behind him someone was speaking slowly in a deep, rough voice that he did not recognise. The surgery was in near darkness. The pen lay by his hand. In front of him on the desk was a flurry of prescription sheets covered in his own scribbled notes. To the side was Malachy's book. The room was filled with an overpowering smell of decaying fish. The back of the doctor's neck tingled. The voice spoke only five words.

"The One will help you."

The doctor felt the hairs rising on his neck, and a hollow sensation in his abdomen. He could not move. Then he heard a rhythmic crackling, mingled with scuffling sounds, moving away from him. He swivelled in his chair, in time to see the back view of a small but solidly built figure walking out through the door. The man was clad in rough dark brown robes with a sash tied round the waist, and tattered leather sandals that brushed the floor as he walked. His head was bald at the centre.

The hairs on the doctor's neck resumed their usual angle of inclination. He quickly got up and walked to the door, opened it and looked out; there was no one to be seen. He came back into the room, still full of fishy aroma, and stood still, turning over in his mind the words that had been spoken. Then he walked out to the pantry that served as archival storage. The message left by his unsolicited visitor echoed round his head.

Somewhere in the depths of his memory resonated a faint signal of recognition, something that he couldn't quite bring to the surface. He'd heard something about 'The One' before - but when? Dr. O'Toole stood thinking. Then he remembered - it was a turn of phrase the oldest folks had used once in a while when he was very young. They'd speak about it and look at each other in a peculiar way, and if you asked what they were talking about they'd say you'd have to ask the real old-timers, *the Ancients* as they called them. At the time it had seemed like a sort of mysterious game. He'd asked his father what was that game they were playing and he said it wasn't a game, it was serious; but he needn't worry about it, not yet for a year or two at least, maybe he would explain some day when his son was older. He hadn't said at the time that maybe he'd have to be sixty years older to find out.

So every now and again he would ask his father if he was old enough to know about it, but his father never told him. And then he'd stopped asking, because he'd started to find out about other things with the help of the local girls, and he'd got more interested in that. And by the time he got interested in the other thing again his father was gone.

That was why he eventually got into writing the archives. Of course he had the Inishower gene in him, so he had to be writing about something, but he was no good at making up his own stories. So he'd just write down things people said and things people did, and then things he could remember from when he was younger. He saved up all his bits of writing, and before he knew it he was the island's historical expert. And then he'd married Molly and it suited him to continue with it, as a handy escape activity. And it sort of grew on him.

So now Dr. O'Toole looked along the densely piled shelves for his very earliest records - notes that went back fifty years or more. Then he found it: a file called *The Ancients*. The folder itself was disintegrating, but the notes were still legible - on Inishower they knew a thing or two about using paper and ink that endured; for the most valuable possession that an Inishovian could pass down to the offspring would be the writings. Most other material possessions, apart from knitting needles of course, were considered more or less worthless.

The doctor stood there till he had read a thick fistful of the yellowed handwritten pages; then he smiled to himself and put them away. He must have written this stuff all those years ago without having any clue what it meant. Now it was making sense. It was time to pay a visit to the Ancients of Wiscoyle.

It had been a very long time since Dr. O'Toole had visited the tiny lake of Wiscoyle[5]. For a start, he never went on uphill treks any more. He hadn't realised that anyone actually lived out there; but the notes claimed that somebody certainly did. Wiscoyle nestled close up to the mountain, and most folks felt uncomfortable even taking a walk up there, never mind settling down to live. There were many old stories about the lake, and in none of them did anyone live happily ever after.

Wiscoyle was a small, black and deep tarn set in a corrie on the lower slopes of Mount Eireaball, gouged out by glacial action in the last ice age. According to local legend it was created by the giant mythological hero-writer Finn McScreed. Finn was renowned for the great epic poems he wrote about his own fictitious heroic exploits, as well as his prodigious capacity for taking intoxicating liquor.

In the latter part of his life the drink, which had once stimulated his creative faculties, was having the opposite effect, and he was unable to come up with any new ideas for his own exploits. So with great strides he would wander restlessly over the Celtic homelands, stepping over mountains and across seas and seeking inspiration; until one day he came wading over to the small island of Inishower for the day. He'd been drinking particularly heavily and badly needed to empty his bladder. Now McScreed was unnaturally fastidious about such matters, and was unable to urinate in any but the proper place. It was too far to go back to his own facilities in the

---

[5] Formally known as Lochan Uisciuil, literally the Little Watery Lake

Alpine lakes, so he looked around for a hole in the ground. Finding none, he quickly scooped out a hollow near the base of the mountain on which he'd been sitting, and used that; and it's said that the debris of shards and splinters of rock that he pulled out and threw over the far side of the mountain formed the Devil's Quills that stand at the bottom of the Cliffs of Manachleim.

It was certainly true that the lake to this day possessed a distinctive odour consistent with this imaginative telling of its origins. It was also held locally that the waters of this magical lake were wetter than normal water; the traditional view was that they could not drain away and so had become more and more concentrated. And so the lake was regarded as the most potent of all the waters of Inishower for scrying - gazing into its surface to foresee the future and access the past. But the dangers inherent in this activity were great, because anyone who fell in the lake would never be able to dry off. Prolonged immersion meant that you would never get rid of the smell; so you would lose your friends and no one would be willing to have sexual relations with you; you'd have no children, die out as a family line, and generally have a very bad time in life.

All in all, then, the people of Inishower had good reason not to go near Wiscoyle Loch; but Dr. O'Toole didn't have the luxury of a choice in the matter. One other thing that he had gleaned from his notes bothered him too: that you were only ever allowed one trip to the Ancients. What did that mean - that you died as soon as you met them? Or that they killed you? Did they perhaps serve up poisonous cups of tea, or maybe lethal biscuits? These were the kind of thoughts that ran through the doctor's mind as he dragged his unwilling bulk up the lower slopes of the mountain in the twilight. A misty drizzle completely consumed the upper reaches. His breath grew short, and he perspired copiously into his heavy woollen tweeds; their natural wicking could not cope with the dampness he was experiencing from without and within. This was work for a younger man than himself, he thought.

At last he struggled over a steep rise and there was the small lake ahead of him, nestling back against the mountain side - black, unrippled and not smelling good at all. But he could see no houses; indeed there was no sign of life anywhere. No birds could be heard; no fish or swimming insect broke the mirror-like surface of the dark water; and round the margins there was a marked absence of the lush vegetation that characterised every other part of the island. He walked closer to the lake, keeping well back from the acrid water's edge; he scanned the surroundings for some semblance of a habitation. The mist was growing denser and the light dimmer. Then he noticed a speck of light amongst a dense bank of ferns and creepers right against the face of the mountain, on the far side of the water. He moved towards it round the bare shore, keeping his eyes on that point lest he should lose his bearing.

Now he saw that the light was emanating from behind dense vegetation that completely covered the rising side of the mountain itself - a small rainforest of undergrowth spreading up the steep slope above, sending down a steady cascade of dripping moisture. He drew closer. A greenish glimmer was coming from some sort of window set into the rock face. But if this was the dwelling, where was the door? He couldn't see any such thing in the gathering gloom.

"Hello?" he called out. Nothing happened. He called again, louder this time. Still nothing. Maybe the Ancients weren't in. Or maybe, if they were so very old, they were also hard of hearing. He yelled this time at the top of his voice, right outside the window, which he could now see was covered in grime and green mould.

"Hello! Is there anybody there?"

This time he heard a stirring from within, and then a faint slushy sound as if someone was dragging wet blankets to and fro across a floor. The source of the sound seemed to draw closer. A silhouetted head appeared dimly behind the opaquely coated window.

"It's him," said a high, thin voice. "He's here." And the head withdrew from behind the window. Then the wet blanket resumed its rhythmic sweeping, moving behind the vegetation. Next thing there was a rattling, and part of the foliage-covered canopy to the left of the doctor began to shake. Another rattle and bang, and a section of the foliage pushed outwards, then settled back. Muffled cursing was heard from within. A third thud, and the panel moved a bit more. This was followed by more swearing and evident discontent; then a solid upright rectangular segment of vegetation began to swing out towards him; apparently this was the door. As the gap opened, a parcel of excessively humid air with a distinctly urinal tang engulfed the doctor. But the enshrouding tendrils of ivy ferns growing in front of the door still held it back.

"Give it a good yank there, young fellow," came the voice again through the gap. The doctor grasped the edge of the door and pulled. The protagonist on the other side kicked at it, the ferns and tendrils yielded and tore, and the door swung fully open. Another wave of hot, damp atmosphere washed over the doctor. He stepped into the open doorway, his head a little light.

The scene before him was dimly lit by a single, sputtering lamp placed near the back of a small cave-like room; it must have been carved back into the side of the mountain, or perhaps eroded over time by the action of water. For everything was exceedingly wet. Moisture dripped from the ceiling, and small rivulets glistened as they ran this way and that over the dark floor. Two smallish people were within, one standing and one sitting down. The one before him wore a thick tweed jacket and dark green baggy trousers. He stood bent over a stick, looking up at the doctor. The other figure sat to the right in a chair made of sticks that had leaves growing out of them; she was wearing a long sea-green woollen skirt-like garment; she must be the wife and knitting some sort of shapeless dark thing. Both were thin, and both looked very wet. Their clothes were wet; their hair was wet; their wrinkled skin was wet. As an Inishovian the doctor was used to dampness in the home, but this was unusual. And from the smell that came off them he wondered if they bathed in the lake daily; one visit to the Ancients, he could see, would be more than enough. Damp though they were, the eyes of both were bright and lively within their shrivelled faces.

The room was sparsely furnished. On the left was a desk with a pen, some purple parchment and a bottle of bright blue ink, and a chair; all the furniture seemed to be made of the wood that was full of life and sprouting. A third chair sat in the middle, facing towards the door. The back wall of the space was of dark green moss-covered rock, with another door set into it, perhaps leading further into the mountain. He couldn't see any sign of tea or biscuits.

"You'll be young Ulick O'Toole," said the man. "Come on in out of the wet."

"I am," said the doctor, entering.

"What's that?" asked the man, leaning closer to him.

"I am Ulick O'Toole!" shouted the doctor towards him, overpowered once more by the smell.

"What's taken you so long?" asked the woman. Her voice was higher and thinner still than the man's, with a bit of hoarseness in it as well. But her hearing seemed better; she would be the one to talk to. The doctor moved closer to her. His own feet were already doing the wet blanket noise.

"So you've been expecting me?" said the doctor.

"What?" said the man.

"We have," said the woman. "Take a seat."

"How long for?" asked the doctor.

"About forty years," she said. She nodded her head towards the man.

"I told him you'd be here," she went on, "but he wouldn't listen. There's no telling him."

"What's that?" said the man. The woman ignored him. If the Ancients had been old forty years ago, the doctor wondered, what age must they be now? The man gave up on the conversation and swished over to the desk.

"Do you know what I'm here for, then?" he asked the woman.

"Oh yes, indeed," she said. "It's our business to know these things. Once in a while somebody comes by and needs something. Usually it's St. Scombrel that sends them." She paused and laughed.

"That St. Scombrel," she went on. "He was a scallywag. He did a good deal of preaching and healing and that sort of thing in his time, but he was really only interested in doing good works on the women." She paused again, and smiled. "Sure he couldn't keep that prong to himself. He said it was his healing tool. And he certainly did a lot of healing with it. Mind you, the menfolk of his day weren't so pleased." She looked over at her husband. "But Scombrel didn't bother about that."

Nice idea, thought the doctor. The penis as a healing tool. Worth bearing in mind for later.

"Oh yes," she continued, "He was a scamp all right. And he had a fierce tongue on him; he said it was part of the beauty of creation. You could have learnt a lot of dirty, filthy language from a man like that. But he had a good heart." She paused again, as if recalling fond memories.

"Anyway, he doesn't often send anyone," she said. "Only when there's a reason. Otherwise life is fairly quiet here. I do the scrying, Oran does the scrudging. It passes the time, you know."

"*Scrudging*?" said the doctor. "Oran can do *scrudging*?" He noticed that the man was now at his desk, writing with the bright blue ink.

"Oh yes, he's always done it. But he's not very good at it. He scrudges some peculiar things sometimes." She spoke here in a quieter voice, as if that was going to make any difference. "He's getting on in years now, you know. And sometimes he gets up to a bit of mischief."

"Mischief?" said the doctor. "You mean with events on the island?"

"Indeed, I wouldn't put that past him. But of course he'd always have a good reason. It would be for your own good."

"So Oran could sort out Malachy for us, with *scrudging*?" said the doctor.

"Oh no, we wouldn't be allowed to do that. You have to work it out for yourself. We can only point you in the right direction.

"So what's the right direction?" asked the doctor. "What do we have to do to put an end to all this trouble with Malachy?"

"I can't tell you what to do. I can only give you certain information."

"So what's the information that we need?"

"You have to ask me questions. Then I can give you answers; that's how it works."

"What kind of questions?"

"Questions to which there are three answers," she said.

The doctor frowned. This was something he'd not heard about.

"So what did you come here to find out?" asked the woman. The doctor thought.

"I came to find out about 'The One'. Who is 'The One'?"

"I cannot answer you that; there's only one answer. Ask me another question."

The doctor thought about this. He couldn't ask directly who The One was; but maybe he could ask about it in another way. What kind of question would have three answers?

"What are three things I need to know about The One?" he ventured.

"Ah," the woman replied. She closed her eyes and cleared her throat. When she continued her voice was in an altogether lower register.

"I can answer you that. It is said of old that there are three masteries that characterise The One. These shall be: the mastery of the mackerel, the mastery of the mystical and the mastery of minstrelsy. Thus is the threefold saying of old." Her voice went back up to normal pitch. "So there you are," And then she added, "but I should tell you that you have to be careful of imitations."

What did that mean, the doctor wondered? He turned over other possible questions in his mind. How about this one, then:

"What is it that The One will do for us?"

"I cannot answer you that." Was that because it's only one thing that's to be done, or more than three things? She couldn't answer that either; of course not - there'd only be one answer. It wasn't going very well. Then the doctor decided to try a long shot.

"What would you say are the three ways that The One might be recognised?" To his relief the woman's face went into happy-to-be-able-to-help-you mode.

"I can answer you that," she said, her eyes closing and her voice going down a couple of octaves. "It is said of old that The One shall possess the three peculiarities of the *physical* variety…" - she emphasised that word as if to indicate a slight bending of the rules here - "…known as the Three Paradoxical Stigmata of St. Scombrel, which are as follows: though flexible of mind and spirit, The One shall possess stiffness of body; though not of an island race, The One shall possess saltiness of the blood; though not of this island race, The One shall possess the Prong of Inishower. Thus is the threefold saying of old."

"Aha!" cried the doctor. "So The One is a he and not a she?"

"I cannot answer you that." Of course not - there'd only be one answer. All the same, it seemed a fair bet.

By the time the doctor left, he was wringing water out of his clothes and out of his hair and out of his skin, now white and wrinkled like an albino prune. By the end of the session - the only session, presumably - he'd got the hang of it. He'd worked out that as long as he wasn't asking questions about the central matter that he'd come about, his confidante would grow voluble on a wide variety of matters; she probably just appreciated a bit of company and somebody that could hear what she was saying. At times she lapsed into praising the old days with nostalgia, bemoaning recent centuries when people had been far too busy trying to do more than three things in one lifetime. On the off chance, the doctor took the opportunity to ask why the number three was so important; and she gave him three very good reasons.

But by not asking questions at all the doctor learned even more. He gathered a great deal about St. Scombrel and his times, and what he'd got up to in those days. All in all, it was highly illuminating. And as the wife was speaking, the doctor observed the man Oran writing very slowly in a bright blue spidery scrawl on the purple paper, over at his jungle of a desk. But the moment the doctor finally got up to go, Oran put his pen back in the glass inkwell and stopped writing.

Now all the doctor had to do was confirm who The One was; and of course he had a fairly shrewd idea. There was just the one physical criterion that he needed to check up on to make absolutely sure; and surely that couldn't be too difficult.

It was pitch black outside. Pleased to find himself still alive and completely unpoisoned by tea or biscuits, the doctor picked his way round the lake by sense of smell alone, and proceeded down the slope to the bog road and on home. As soon as he got there he wrote down all he'd learned that evening.

The Golden Age

In the history of Inishower, the Celtic Christian era represents perhaps the finest flowering of religion, arts and culture. Yet it also presents to the observer the most unexpected and seemingly contradictory elements.

It is well known that Inishower was Christianised in the late fourth century AD, ahead of mainland Ireland and the Scottish isles by Scombrel, the island's celebrated patron saint. We know that St. Scombrel lived the early part of his life somewhere in the Mediterranean area and that as a youth he herded sheep in winter and fished the sea in summer, until captured by seafaring Inishovian Celtic warriors who brought him back to their homeland. Here he worked as a slave tending the flocks and fishing, for flock-tending and sea-fishing skills were scarce in their culture, focused as it was on writing and literary conquest. It transpired that the young Scombrel also had innate powers of healing, and an ability to manifest salt from his body that was regarded as miraculous. Scombrel rose quickly through society by virtue of this unique combination of attributes. In the course of doing so he is said to have converted to his own faith every woman that he met; their husbands had no choice but to follow suit. Thus grew Scombrel's reputation as a missionary and charismatic spiritual leader.

Scombrel was also instrumental in developing modern writing on the island. In the pre-Christian era, carved stone message slabs on Inishower had progressively become thinner and lighter, until a cluster of them could be hinged together with leather thongs to form the precursor of the 'book'. But it was under Scombrel's supervision that the next step was taken. Using quills from the now extinct Inishower Purple Swan, dyes from the Bog Inkwort and vellum made from native sheepskin, modern writing was introduced to the island.

Before long the charismatic Scombrel had set up a monastery, featuring a unique form of non-reclusive monasticism.

He promoted recording of old Celtic poems, myths and legends, and study of pre-Christian spirituality. He trained many of the native islanders as writer-monks and sent them off as missionaries to convert the rest of the British Isles. Scombrel himself also travelled widely, always alone in a tiny boat, and is said to have voyaged far and wide in his attempts to set up writing classes all over Ireland. The monastery produced many fine illuminated manuscripts on the Inishower vellum, known as the most durable writing medium in the ancient world. These pages were bound into great volumes whose beauty we can now only imagine.

All this has been known for some time. But our picture has only recently been revolutionised by significant discoveries about St. Scombrel and his heritage, running counter to the pattern of Christian civilisation in the remainder of Europe. St Scombrel, it seems, did not match the stereotypical standards of the conventional abbot.

For a start, Scombrel promoted a quite distinctive view of the realm of the spiritual. He taught that the divinity had three archetypal aspects - the shepherd who cared for the flock, the fisherman who provided spiritual sustenance, and the author-creator who wrote life into existence. This concept irrevocably influenced the culture of Inishower, which to this day embraces in daily life the corresponding 'holy trinity' of writing, knitting and mackerel. And this notion was supported by the law of Triads, a local custom that required everything to be expressed in threes. Even now the rule of threes is applied in literary construction irrespective of genre, throughout the island.

Most controversial, though, has been the recent revelation that St. Scombrel was not the ascetic previously thought. It now appears that a great deal of heathen shamanism and Eastern mysticism found its way into Inishower monasticism, including fondness for the fertility rituals in which Scombrel himself liked to play a central role. Typical of these was the ceremony of Tortulacht *where he would appear clad only in the* ronnachbod [6] *and perform intimate rites with three vestal virgins. Such was Scombrel's ardour said to be that he would occasionally need to cool it by making epic voyages to icy regions such as Greenland and Newfoundland. Scombrel was also the earliest Irish authority on tantric sexual practices, and fond of penning erotic haiku. In his own time he was sometimes referred to as Scombrel the Stiff, but it is not known whether this referred to a general or specific physical attribute. For it is now believed that the great saint suffered from the little known condition known as* Sclerosis Saliensis *or de Beauvoir's disease, characterised by the tendency to exude copious amounts of salt from the skin. After death, his body is said to have resisted decomposition for hundreds of years, taken as evidence of holiness that did much for his spiritual reputation in the following centuries.*

More surprising still is what is now known about the nature of the great books produced under St. Scombrel's supervision. Most renowned among these was the Kelsa Sutra, *a lavishly illustrated guide to the ancient tantric practices. It is believed that all the main Inishower texts of this period were embellished in the margins with ornate erotic sketches and graffiti, drawn by the monks as a tribute to the fecundity of Creation. The* Kelsa Sutra *is said to still exist, allegedly hidden away for some fifteen centuries in a secret cavern deep within Mount Eireaball.*

Less surprisingly, the Inishower approach to Christianity did not catch on in a big way in the rest of Ireland and Europe; yet attempts to suppress it on the island invariably failed. Scombrel died peacefully in bed in the year 569 at the age of ninety-eight, in the company of two faithful female consorts, in a complicated sexual position known as Flying Ducks Reversed.

U.o'T.

---

[6] Literally *'penile mackerel mask'*

24 Prongitude

Dr. O'Toole slept long, deep and late after completing his nocturnal reconstruction work on the archival records. His only dream was a relatively entertaining one about St. Scombrel, who was told by a booming voice from heaven that tremendous rain and a devastating flood were on the way; whereupon the diligent saint built a big boat and loaded it with three of every kind of animal on earth including women but not men, and floated off towards the horizon having a terrific time. The doctor lay on in bed, recalling yesterday evening's escapade and wondering how to get the final point of confirmation that he needed. Today was a very big day in the festival, with the presentation of the island's annual literary awards; he'd have to get it sorted before any of that began. In fact, he'd have to start working on it right away.

Dr. O'Toole looked out through his small bedroom window; quite a nice light sleety rain was falling with little evidence of wind, and around the house someone had cleared up the festooning fibres of yesterday: Niamh, probably. Then, to his surprise, the most welcome of Inishower culinary aromas greeted his nostrils and brought him quickly out of bed and down to the kitchen.

The *scrivlin* was hanging up to the right of the fire-place, which was the custom when such an item was finished but not yet worn. Captain Flaherty was seated at the table; Niamh was shovelling two fat mackerel onto the plate in front of him - a clean picked carcass on another plate showed that she'd already eaten. Her cheeks had a touch of colour in them and the cleft seemed to be at a relatively safe level.

"Good morning, doctor," said Captain Flaherty.

"Good morning to you both," replied the doctor. "Have you seen the book they brought back from..."

"Don't talk to me about Malachy Moodie!" interrupted Niamh, turning on her father. "When I get a hold of that man I'll put a distance between himself and his testicles. Somebody had better bring him in, and soon." Then she turned to the captain, and the cleft seemed to drop again.

"Will you have another fish?" she asked.

"Ah no, Niamh, thanks," he replied. "These'll be fine."

"There's some for you, then," she said to the doctor, and put a new one in the pan. "You'll be needing it to get down to business and have that Malachy brought in."

Niamh fried the fish and the doctor ate it without risking another word. When the captain had finished eating, the doctor thought he'd invite him out for a walk and a chat on the bog road, and maybe bring up the subject of physiological peculiarities; but then he had a better idea. Why not get somebody else to do the job? Somebody, perhaps, who already had a proven interest in the subject?

Five minutes later Dr. O'Toole donned his coat and left the house by himself; and as he did so he heard the sound of Captain Flaherty beginning to play on his instrument. And the doctor might have been mistaken, but it didn't seem to be coming from the surgery on the ground floor, but from one of the upstairs windows. And he could have been wronger still, but he also thought he heard a bit of his daughter's laughter mixed in with it. But he put it out of his mind, focusing instead on a work assignment that he'd just thought up for Sally-Anne Peachley at the masterclass - a follow-up piece of investigative journalism and fieldwork which he knew would be close to her heart or other intimate organs.

In gossipy circles on the Irish mainland it is sometimes quipped that the best way to advertise anything is to pass the word round that it's a secret. On Inishower things were a little different, for the literary curiosity and the collective psyche were so highly developed and finely tuned that the best way to get something known about was to keep it to yourself and not tell anybody at all.

And so it was that when Dr. O'Toole had finished his class and then stepped into McDadgh's to make plans for the evening's ceremonies and catch up on the crack, the place went completely quiet - for perhaps the second or third time in its history. The doctor thought it odd indeed, but wrote that down to resentment over not having done enough to bring Malachy to justice. Consequently, as soon as he'd finished making his arrangements he thought he'd leave. The minute he'd gone, the gossip and speculation picked up right where it had left off; and it wasn't about Malachy or the terrorism book or any of that stuff. It was about something a little more up to date:

"Is it him, do you think, Brian? Is he The One?"

"It might be him. What do you think, Dierdre?"

"I'd say it might be him. I can't think of anybody else. What do you say, Fergus?"

"I was thinking the very same thing meself, Dierdre. But what about the apparatus?"

"That's the thing. Has he got the apparatus?"

"That's the very thing I was wondering."

"You're right there, Michael."

"Aye."

"Indeed."

Interest in the topic was rife, even by Inishower standards. The women were interested in it. The men were interested in it. And not just the locals - the de Boyle set, having managed to find out what 'it' was, were extremely interested, although they had little idea of its ultimate significance. Everybody wanted to know. Everyone wanted to be absolutely sure.

"Well all I can say is, it had better be him."

"You're right there."

"Indeed."

It was an unheard of thing for Dr. O'Toole to get to the pub and not spend the long form of the afternoon there. But having curtailed his stay on this occasion, he was soon on his way back to the house. He thought that maybe, after all, he would do an extra bit of research on the captain for himself. But the man wasn't to be found in the surgery, nor in the kitchen nor out the back, nor anywhere that he could see. Neither was Niamh; nor was the knitted *scrivlin*. Then the doctor spotted an empty whiskey bottle and two glasses on the table.

The doctor put the kettle on and wondered what to do next, at which point he thought he could hear sounds from upstairs. He quietly opened the door to the stair and listened. The muffled voice of Niamh was coming from her room, with occasional contributions from Captain Flaherty. The doctor made his way carefully up the stair avoiding the bad step that creaked, and then hovered outside her door, ready to dart straight into his own room in the event of an emergency. Whatever was going on sounded remarkably light-hearted, which might have had something to do with the drink. Niamh was doing most of the talking. Her voice was slurred and interspersed with frequent giggling, such as he hadn't heard from the girl since well before she'd met Malachy.

"Ah go on," she was saying. "You have to try it on, it's finished now, sure I need to see how it fits." The doctor heard her walk across the room. The captain seemed to assent.

"Here it is," she said. "Isn't it fucking marvellous?" She seemed to think this remark very funny.

"It is indeed very very marvellous," agreed the captain, and he too thought it funny; seemingly he had had his share of the whiskey. "I've never seen a marvellouser thing in my life, which has been very very full of marvellousness." They both laughed again.

"Here you are then," said Niamh. "Take off them things and try it on."

"Take off what things?" the captain asked.

"All them things," said Niamh. "It's traditional, you have to do it; sure you can't do the first fitting of the *scrivlin* with anything on. And anyway, I've got to burn your old things, they're terrible awful." She giggled again.

This conversation was followed by assorted sounds of movement and fabric and joint laughter, and then silence of the sort you hear when two people are getting as close as they possibly can and they're wondering what's going to happen next. The doctor still stood, listening. He would say that he tried to drag himself away, but he didn't. He told himself he was only there for what he needed to know. It was for the good of the community; the future of the island was at stake. So that was all right then.

Now there was another sustained bout of miscellaneous scufflings, and more laughing from both sides. Then it went quiet again - very quiet - followed by breathing through the nose that wasn't getting any lighter, the mouths presumably being otherwise occupied. Then bed-spring sounds started coming into it, without words or laughter; it was getting serious. This continued for what seemed like a couple of minutes…

"Hang on a minute," he suddenly heard Niamh say, and barefooted feet slapped across the room; the doctor instantly dived through his own bedroom doorway. But Niamh's door didn't stir; instead there was the sound of a drawer opening and closing again within; more footslaps; then a rustling that the doctor recognised well from times well past.

"You'll have to put this on," said Niamh, "but I don't know whether it'll work on you." Fumbling noises, and then Niamh was bursting with laughter again.

"It fits! It fits!" she shrieked.

"So it would seem," came the voice of the captain.

At this point the doctor finally crept down the stairs, as rhythmic bedspring creakings established themselves within the room. Niamh and the captain: a satisfying blend of acid and alkaline, he thought. And he reckoned he had all the verification he needed. Maybe he would take that walk on the bog road, and decide what was to be done next.

He went into the hall and put on his tweedwool coat. But as he opened the back door, he was surprised to hear a sudden clattering sound coming from round the side of the house. He stepped outside cautiously, tiptoed to the corner, and peered round. There was nothing to be seen; but the same noise was now to be heard from the front. Then it went quiet. Holding his breath he crept along the house wall till he came to the next corner, and poked his head round. About a hundred yards away from the house, running down the road towards the village, was the lithe figure of Sally-Anne Peachley clutching a ladder. The doctor laughed; that girl certainly took her fieldwork seriously.

He strode round to the back of the house again and down the path to the back gate. A lovely light drizzle was falling, and there was no wind at all. It was a peculiarly good feeling that he had. And as he turned onto the bog road he could hear on the still air something he hadn't heard for a while. In his daughter's voice from the upstairs window of his house came repetitive utterance of that short affirmative adverb traditionally favoured in satisfactory sexual encounters. Yes, the doctor thought to himself; it sounds like he's the one all right.

25 What Have the Roman-a-clefs Ever Done for Us?

Dr. O'Toole made sure he stayed out long enough to avoid interrupting his daughter and her guest. He walked the bog road around the three sides of the mountain and back, fully aware that Malachy was somewhere up there and that something had to be done about it.

When he returned to the house at dusk Niamh and Captain Flaherty were in the kitchen. The air in the room was easier to walk into than for some time. The captain was wearing the mackerel *scrivlin*, and there was no sign at all of the Cleft of Inishower to be seen on any part of his daughter. A reading of nil on Niamh: the doctor had never seen that - she'd even been born with a wee bit of a cleft; it had been the first thing he'd checked, even before is-it-a-boy-or-is-it-a-girl? Nor could he ever recall a nil reading on her mother, come to think of it; so what did that mean?

More surprises ensued; Niamh greeted her father with some warmth and put the kettle on for him; her speech was still somewhat slurred. The captain was even quieter than usual, though possibly harbouring a hint of a smile. Inscrutable was the word that came into the doctor's mind; that man had less scrutes than anyone he could think of. The doctor complemented the garment and its creator, and then no one knew what to say; Niamh started giggling. Records were tumbling all over the place. Then she suggested that the three of them go down early for the awards at McDadgh's; and she went off to get dressed for the occasion.

Niamh returned in her finest red wool frock. The doctor got out his best suit, which he hadn't worn for ten years or more; and the captain stayed in his vivid *scrivlin*. Five minutes later they all set off down the road; the doctor noticed that Niamh's arm was in the captain's, and it was still there as they walked into McDadgh's.

The roar that came from the place as the doctor opened the door evaporated as they stepped in. All eyes were on the captain, though maybe with different thoughts. For as soon as they were inside, a host of knitting wives swooped down on the multicoloured individual, who disappeared into the midst of the buzzing swarm. The knitters' eyes were fixed on the garment, but the comments were addressed to Niamh who stood nearby with the air of the cat that got two lots of cream.

"How did you do that bit of intarsia, Niamh?"

"Where did that cable pattern come from?"

"I didn't know we had that colour..."

"How on earth did you get that silver sheen?"

"Fancy that for an axis stitch!"

"I've never seen a loose sloped bind-off loop used like that..."

"Look at those invisible cast-ons, would you!"

They closed in further, poking this and pulling that and turning back hems, clicking and clucking in their excitement and checking gussets in intimate regions.

"Nice bit of splicing down there, Niamh."

"Lovely ease allowances."

"That'll give him some protection all right."

"Doesn't he wear it well?"

"You'd swear he was one of our folk."

"Your mother would be proud of you, Niamh."

And then the final collective summary chorus, in a rare vein of feminine sentimentality that their menfolk might not hear for another long while:

"Ah Niamh, its *gorgeous*!"

And the swarm shifted its focus to Niamh, dragging her off to the lounge bar, ostensibly to winkle out of her the trade secrets of her knitting but more importantly to get the low-down on the captain's no-longer-private parts.

With the ruckus of knitters out of the way the background swell of pub noise quickly got back up to a respectable level, and the next priority could be attended to - the build-up to the business of the annual awards. Excitement was intense, for it was always the best attended event of the festival. The place was already packed, and more punters were arriving by the minute.

Inishower festival had never bothered with the dull, routine, run-of-the-mill kind of awards that you could find elsewhere on the literary circuit; the doctor saw to that. He also displayed an unswerving predilection for prizes which the people of Inishower were likely to win. The so-called Inishower Open Poetry Competition, for instance, was invariably won by a local because it only accepted epic poems in which the hero is a mackerel. Likewise the Ursula Dryppe Memorial Prize for a novel that describes the weather conditions in detail in every single scene; and the Howard G. Scrank Scholarship to write a work about spiders that live in damp climates – no one other than islanders had ever applied for these. There was also a whole range of awards within the genre of 'saturation comedy', which no one outside Inishower had even heard of.

So the awards naturally attracted the kind of controversy that can help such enterprises a good deal. Only a couple of years ago Dervla Dunphy, disgruntled runner-up in the Inishower Crime Writers Association Golden Dagger Award, had grabbed the coveted prize and used it to fatally stab the winner. And in the twenty years since the inception of the Agnes Frumpe Prize for the most reclusive writer on the island, it had never once been claimed by its recipient; with this kind of precedent, any future winner that turned up to receive it would probably have to be automatically disqualified. This sort of thing added to the appeal of the occasion as far as both locals and visitors were concerned. And since the doctor himself was the judging panel for all the awards, and insisted on shortlists of one name known only to himself, people could assume right up to the last minute that they were in with a chance. Most local authors would write stuff specially for one or other prize; some dedicated souls seemed to spend most of the year on it and enter up to twenty categories.

Everyone, therefore, was awaiting the announcements with equally eager anticipation. Joe Quillory, for instance, fancied his chances this year in the Jeffrey Spite Prize for a very long novel written in revenge against another writer, with his nine hundred page tome, *Seumas Reame is a ****ing *****. And Fran MacDivott was confident of winning the Wool Co-operative Award for a novelette based on the history of knitting. Yet history had shown that things didn't always go the islanders' way. The Iveagh Grosse Bequest for an unpublishable short story by a bisexual author over seventy was often taken by a member of the de Boyle set; so the whole clan was out in their finery tonight, almost exploding with sexual excitement.

Such an occasion would not be complete without complaints, and these mostly emanated from those who had not won. Many quibbled about the doctor going too far in creating unusual prizes, resulting in some that were more or less unawardable. They would cite the Finoula Savage Competition for a play written by an orphan brought up by wild animals, or the Magillicuddy Trophy for an espionage tale penned in invisible ink. The awards were criticised, too, for overly restrictive conditions, such as the uncompromising Ne Plus Endowment for a 'last novel'. There was also the Twilight Award for an erotic novel written in the evenings by someone who worked by day as a door-to-door vacuum cleaner salesperson, and the Paddy Sheugh Garland for an autobiography that contained no adjectives. Several prizes specified unusual or punitive lifestyle restrictions, such as that the winner must 'never set foot on the Irish mainland', or 'spend the winnings in a sunny climate'. But few of these criticisms were pursued for long because the doctor saw to it that everybody won something every now and again, furthering the immense popularity of the occasion - which thus marked the absolute zenith of the doctor's powers in the regular annual cycle.

And he made the most of it now, swanning about as one who might still be swayed in his choice of winner in one category or another right up to the moment of announcement. When the doctor felt that he had milked this to the full, he gave the nod that presentations were about to begin. The word went round quickly, amid last minute chattering speculation. The knitters had now joined their respective writer-spouses, ready to voice belligerent objection should their partners be passed over.

It was at this point that the doctor took it into his mind to come up with a new award on the spur of the moment, designed expressly for Captain Flaherty to win. The captain was obviously a popular figure, clearly subject to additional speculative interest at present. The doctor looked over to where the man still stood near the back in his dazzling outfit. He began to make his way towards him through the densely packed crowd. But on the way he saw that Sally-Anne Peachley had got there first; and the doctor realised the urgent need to convey to her that execution of her investigative project was no longer strictly necessary. But Sally-Anne Peachley was the quick worker as ever and before the doctor could get anywhere near, it was too late.

"That's a fine garment you're wearing," he heard her say to the captain. "I'm so interested in these things. Do you wear anything under it?" Without waiting for a reply, she continued. "And what an interesting piece of detail you have down there," she said, simultaneously pulling back the flap provided for dealing with nature's calls of the secondary kind - and in the same deft movement plunging her hand into the gussetted enclave that lay behind. She was clearly skilled in this kind of manoeuvre.

"Oh!" she gasped melodramatically. "That's interesting. Very interesting indeed." But before she had time to remove her hand, something quick and dark and exceedingly angry had flung itself upon her back. It was Niamh.

"Get your hands off that!" she yelled, grabbing a fistful of Sally-Anne's pretty blond locks and wrenching her head back with considerably more force than was strictly necessary. Sally-Anne screamed.

The crowd immediately shifted round to get a better appraisal of this development. Sally-Anne drew her right hand from the captain's groin and hit Niamh across the left cheek, knocking her bodily sideways. The crowd edged closer, roaring encouragement; the captain was swallowed up in the throng, and the doctor realised to his relief that there was no way he could get through to intervene. Niamh, now yelling and spitting venom, pulled on Sally-Anne's hair till her head came close enough to seize the left ear in her teeth. Sally-Anne shrieked into a higher register and grabbed Niamh's throat. Niamh made a counter-move, putting her strong knitter's fingers into Sally-Anne's mouth and pulling on that. Sally-Anne clawed at Niamh's eyes with her bright red fingernails; Niamh narrowly averted this lunge, leant back and punched Sally-Anne's face with a swing from her powerful right arm. Sally-Anne reeled back, then swung into martial arts mode with a high kick that grazed Niamh's head. Niamh dived in for a close grapple and attempted to wrench Sally-Anne's lovely left bosom from its seating. Something serious would be needed if this fight was going to be stopped.

And something serious was indeed provided. It came in the form of a low shaking rumble that mightn't normally be noticed amid the noise, but in the context of recent events was picked up immediately. The crowd stopped shouting. Sally-Anne paused momentarily in her build-up to a flying kick, and Niamh softened her grip on the breast in hand. Everyone knew something bad had happened.

Outside, innumerable tatters of torn and shredded paper were already beginning to float down from the sky in the midst of a light breezy drizzle. They weren't just any old bits of paper; for between them, these fragments encompassed everything that one man knew about the history and the culture and the spirit and the passion and customs and habits, and the deepest intimate secrets, of all the people of Inishower that had ever lived. They were Dr. O'Toole's archives.

26 The Road Less Tarmacced

By no means all of Dr. O'Toole's house had gone up with the papers; the main damage was to the converted pantry that had housed the precious archives, and the bricks and mortar of this corner of the building were now distributed over an adjacent acre or so of island. It would be impossible to say whether the intention had been to selectively destroy the doctor's most beloved possessions, or if it was a bodged attempt to eradicate the whole house and its occupants. The doctor's inclination was to believe the former, while Niamh leaned towards the latter; so both were just about as upset as they could be. Whatever else Malachy had got away with, as far as the O'Toole clan was concerned, he certainly wasn't going to get away with this.

Needless to say Niamh's cleft was well off the scale, and she was up for setting out towards the mountain there and then. The doctor, though clearly gutted by having to walk back from McDadgh's through a landscape littered with the tattered remnants of his life's work, realised that they had to do better than that; he now knew very well who should go up the mountain after Malachy; and for once he told Niamh that was how it was going to be. Captain Flaherty was willing, and Niamh didn't argue after that. So it was settled; the captain would leave for the mountain at the crack of dawn, and do whatever was necessary to bring Malachy back to face the music.

But in the meantime the doctor had important information to impart to the captain. For this he did not need to consult archived notes, as these were matters that had been etched in his mind since being imparted by his father fifty or sixty years earlier - matters that had long held only theoretical significance, but would now be put to the practical test. They centred on the mountain that had always been so beloved to him.

The Mountain

Sleabh Lasc Eireaball is the single most important physical and spiritual presence on Inishower; one who grasps the essence of the mountain holds the key to all the island's secrets and mysteries. No matter how far back one goes in the island's history, Fishtail Mountain has always been held sacred, and no doubt shall always continue to be so.

Fishtail Mountain is composed of some of the oldest and most durable rock that comes to the surface of our planet, thrown up by the drifting tectonic plates in aeons past, then twisted and shifted and shaped through subsequent ages yet never destroyed. Its stubborn bulk has stood up to the incessant battering swells of ocean storms, creating on its seaward side the Cliffs of Manachleim that drop almost unbroken from the twin peaks to the jagged stacks of the Devil's Quills two thousand feet below, where innumerable wayward ships have come to grief over the centuries.

Positioned exactly at the crossing of St. Scombrel's and St. Michael's ley lines, Mount Eireaball harbours a natural vortex of swirling earth energies, and is said to mark one of the Earth's major power points. One of the many manifestations of this force-field is the mountain's highly unstable local weather system. Sudden and radical temperature inversions combined with localised pockets of negative wind pressure can produce a range of conditions that vary from summer snow to a miniature heat wave, in the space of ten minutes. Certain specialised forms of precipitation fall only on the upper reaches of the mountain and nowhere else on the island; these include a particularly dangerous form of sharply pointed hailstones, sudden impenetrable mists, and a peculiarly greasy drizzle. Few individuals alive today can read the signs and indications of these unpredictable conditions.

In times past, however, people knew much more of these things, for locals did not always stay away from the mountain as they do today. Indeed there has long been a well-established pilgrimage route to the top; but this use of highly ritualised access is hedged about with a strict set of protocols. These have been handed down since the time of St. Scombrel, though they are undoubtedly based on beliefs that are very much older.

The traditional pilgrimage of St. Scombrel began in the lowlands at the now ruined monastery, and proceeded in a clockwise spirallic pattern through the Flushey Glen, up to the holy well, past the hermit's cave, along a narrow path that skirts the cliff, and round to a high point near the peak, known as St. Scombrel's Leap. The three main staging points held great local significance. The holy well is where the mountain sheep are said to come to drink, giving them strength to withstand the fierce weather conditions and rough terrain, and considered a significant factor in producing the wool's extraordinary strength and durability of fibre. The cave was St. Scombrel's personal place of retreat where he would withdraw for long periods with certain carefully chosen acolytes in order to teach them the finer points of his esoteric means of enlightenment. And the highest point on the circuit, between the twin summits, is where the saint is said to have once demonstrated his occult powers by leaping off into the sea far below. Before doing so, the legend relates, Scombrel planted his stout green-thorn staff into the ground, and it sprouted into a venerable tree that is said to flourish still at this spot.

According to tradition, these three stations must be visited in the proper sequence, and certain key items must be placed by the supplicant at each. An offering of island wool is to be made at the holy well; an oblation of mackerel must be placed in the cave; and the holy invocation of St. Scombrel has to be uttered at the eponymous leap. The pilgrim must travel on an empty stomach and carry no belongings other than the offerings and the clothes in which he or she stands. Anyone who does not follow these instructions is liable to incur the curse of the saint, enigmatically expressed in allegory that threatens 'falling permanently from grace' and being 'pierced for eternity by the daggers of one's own arrogance'.

U.o'T.

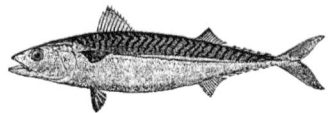

27 A Short Walk and a Windy Push

There weren't many hours of darkness left by the time Dr. O'Toole left Captain Flaherty and retired to his room. When morning came the three of them stood in the kitchen, the captain clad once more in his newly acquired costume. The doctor produced a small object wrapped in black oil-cloth. This, he pronounced, was his most treasured possession, a sacred relic that had been handed down among the males in his family since as long as anyone could remember. It contained a small piece of embalmed mackerel, said to be a fragment of the last meal of St. Scombrel. The doctor was donating this as the offering for the captain to make at St. Scombrel's cave, as a special source of protection and talisman to bring success upon the mission. The captain took the object carefully and stowed it in the depths of his *scrivlin*.

Then Niamh produced her own gift, which she revealed as an heirloom of equal antiquity from the female line of the family. It consisted of a small box carved from a single piece of black bog oak, and she told him that it contained a portion of the revered Inishower Shroud. This was a golden tissue of the finest woollen material ever created on the island, which had been placed over the loins of St. Scombrel after his death, and was said to bear a shadowy imprint of his anatomy. It had never even been seen by a male since coming into the family centuries before. But this was the gift she wished to make to the captain, to present at St. Scombrel's well to further his efforts on behalf of the knitters of Inishower. She placed it gently within the interior of his clothing. Finally the doctor taught Captain Flaherty the text of the secret Invocation of St. Scombrel; and then the captain was on his way.

As he stepped from the house a light dusting of rain fell on him. The land was still dark, but the outline of Mount Eireaball could just be discerned against a lightening sky. Dr. O'Toole's instructions were now imprinted in his mind - every landmark, every feature of the pilgrim's way, every turn in the path. He walked out of the herb garden and turned onto the bog road that curved gently towards the left of the mountain. When he had gone half a mile he turned and looked back. Niamh and the doctor were still standing at the doorway; he turned again and walked on. The road began to rise, and the house was soon out of sight. He was on his way.

Captain Flaherty passed on as the ground grew steeper, strewn now with boulders that had fallen and stayed where they were, for islanders feared to move them. Suddenly he heard above him the sound of rolling rocks and stones; he looked up to where a startled merino ram was dashing away from him to escape intrusion by such vividly coloured strangers.

Soon his path followed the course of the Flushey River as it tumbled down its narrow valley. He paused for a short rest at the foot of a waterfall and observed small speckled trout in the stream, constantly waving their tails to maintain their position in the strong flow. But the captain knew he had to keep his eyes on the slopes above, watching for the dark upright form of Malachy.

As he proceeded upwards the stream grew narrower and steeper still, curving gently all the time round to the right as he climbed. Now it was no more than a series of small cascades that you could easily step over; and after less than half an hour it was just a trickle between the rocks and tufts of damp mountain heather. The captain knew that he was very near its source. He looked ahead, and saw thirty yards on a hollow in the face of the mountain. This must be St. Scombrel's well.

As he drew closer he saw that water was oozing from the interior of the cavity to form a small enclosed circular pool of clear water. The rock behind was almost obscured by lush vegetation that fed on the steady drip and seep of moisture from the spring: dark ferns, vivid cushions of moss and succulent spurges. The captain crouched down inside the hollow, bending over the tiny pool. He pulled from his waist the small black box given him by Niamh. Holding it in one hand, he reached into the foliage in front of him with the other, searching this way and that. Leaning further forward, his arm disappeared into a cavity in the rock. Here he felt a flat shelf, right at the back. Satisfied with this he placed the box within, and then paused a moment in contemplation. If Captain Flaherty had looked behind him exactly then, he would have glimpsed the fleeting presence of a small man dressed in rough robes, who took a quick look at him and then disappeared into the landscape. But the captain didn't look back. He drank a little of the water from the pool, rose carefully, stepped out from the enclosure of the well and stood erect, noticing only a faint fishiness on the air. Then he looked up once more towards the bulk of the mountain above him. Most of it was obscured in rain that was growing heavier now, but he could see the remains of a path that seemed to run up the slope and round it to the right.

As he walked on the foliage grew denser around him, and soon he was in a dripping rainforest of lichen-clad shrubs and gnarled trees hung with damp fronds and creepers. The steep walk was turning into a climb, and he had to grasp at roots and branches to haul himself up. Despite the rain, the day was growing warmer; the *scrivlin* kept in the heat, and he began to perspire.

After almost an hour of tough climbing he emerged from the hillside forest into the open. The rain now seemed to have virtually stopped; it was an odd sensation, one that he had not experienced since coming to Inishower. He stood still and looked around him. The air was still and almost dry; there was not a sound to be heard. His garment was now completely saturated with sweat. He looked towards the mountaintop, where both peaks disappeared into mist. Looking down he could see the whole of the eastern side of the island laid out before him, with the small black lake of Wiscoyle hard up against the mountain, the bogland stretching away towards the village, and the flat eastern beaches beyond.

The landscape ahead was a mixture of rock faces, stunted trees and alpine flowers of brilliant blues and yellows that seemed to flourish in every crevice. But traces of the path could still be discerned between the rocky outcrops, still wending its way upwards; the captain reckoned he was now very near the cave. He began to climb again, and then suddenly stopped. He looked around him carefully, then above and finally below. He strained his eyes, but could see nothing. He began to climb again, but instinctively stopped to look again, and listen. Yet there was no sound, no hint of movement anywhere. He climbed once more, but this time his movements were stealthy and tentative. He tested handholds before putting his weight on them; he avoided bearing down on crumbling rock that would clatter down the mountain and betray his presence. The wind was picking up a little now, but there was still no rain to speak of.

The captain climbed another twenty yards in this way, and began to pull himself up onto a flat green area across which the warm wind rushed from the south, when he saw in front of him the entrance to a cave. He froze for a moment, then called out.

"Malachy!"

Now from the depths of the cave the doctor heard echoing footsteps, and a shambling figure in dark, shredded clothing suddenly appeared at the entrance, looking towards him from under a shock of matted black hair that tossed this way and that in the strong wind. The figure stood still for an instant, then turned and ran to the left of the cave and began to climb the steep jumble of rocks and scree that led up the mountainside from there.

Captain Flaherty heaved himself onto the grassy platform and ran after Malachy. By the time he got to the cave mouth, Malachy was only five lengths of his body up the slope. The captain began to climb. Then he stopped; he realised he could not follow. He watched Malachy disappear soon enough into the mist, never looking back. The captain climbed back down, and entered the cave.

As soon as he crossed the threshold the air was completely still and quiet. He looked around him. He could see that the cave went far back into the mountainside; it had a flat floor, and the sides merged into the roof to form a kind of ribbed vault that diminished in height towards the back. Spirallic carved markings and incised shapes of crosses adorned the side walls between the vertical ribs.

And in the centre of the space lay a jumble of sundry modern items - various tools, clothing that looked unwashed and a number of canisters of different sizes embellished with warning signs. As the captain walked further back into the space, unsavoury odours informed him of unsavoury usage.

His eyes were accustoming themselves to the darkness, and he made his way further and further back, stooping down as the roof grew lower. As the roof closed in on him he was obliged to continue on all fours, and finally to crawl. But still the tunnel grew smaller, until the captain felt he could move no further, and was in complete darkness. At this point he observed that the air surrounding his head was cooler than that behind him. He retreated a little and then advanced again with his left arm and shoulder ahead of him, till he was stuck again. Feeling around with his forward hand, he gathered that the space ahead of him opened out; he appeared to be wedged in a narrow opening between two spaces. Gaining traction with the left hand, he pulled hard; one shoulder and then the other came through. He scrambled forwards, got onto all fours, and then felt round in the dark for the shape of this new chamber. The air here seemed fresh, dry and cool. He could feel the side wall, but not the top. He stood up tentatively; reaching above his head he could now touch the roof. Moving round systematically and making large arcs with his extended arms, the captain worked out that he must be in a hemispherical space that you could just about lie down in at full stretch. The floor was covered with a thick layer of loose fibres that may once have been wool.

Now that the captain's body was not blocking the opening, a little light was filtering through from the cave entrance. He could discern rough carvings on the walls - primitively depicted figures in pairs and in groups, all in explicit procreative positions, as well as many separate and free-standing tapered phallic representations. This must be the inner sanctum that Dr. O'Toole had told him to find; this was where he should leave his offering. He placed it amongst the fibres at the centre of the space, then paused for a moment before turning and making his way back through the opening. If he had instead turned immediately, he might have briefly glimpsed at that moment the image of the small man in the rough robes, peering through from the main part of the cave and then disappearing again just as quickly as before.

When the captain tackled again the narrow opening he had even more difficulty pulling himself through; and as he walked through the main cave, wondering again if he could detect a slight odour of unfresh fish, he noticed that his joints were stiffening for the first time in over a week. He put this down to the cramped position he'd been in; but as he left the outer cave and picked his way up the ever steeper rock face where Malachy had disappeared, he found that his limbs were seizing up still further. Almost immediately he came to a section where the path narrowed down to almost nothing, with the cliff face above and below; he turned himself sideways, pressed against the face of the mountain and edged along, inches at a time. Then he was across.

The path now spiralled tightly round again to the right, and the wind died down as he moved again into the lea of the mountain. Mist began to swirl about him and he knew that he could not be far from the top, yet could not see any sign of it. He pressed on. Then the cloud cleared momentarily and he glimpsed Malachy not far above him; he was climbing slowly, like a man exhausted and with nowhere to go. The mist closed in again, and the captain made an extra effort, dragging himself up from one foothold to the next. His joints were now crackling audibly, but he pushed on harder. Now the air was completely still and the vapour more dense. Soon he heard another sound: the breath of a human being, coming from above - breathing heavily; and also the sound of foot slipping on loose rock. Stones immediately fell around him; the source of the sound was certainly close. The captain climbed as quietly as he could, but was not able to suppress the sounds of his own body. Then he noticed that the terrain was changing again; the climb was getting easier, the incline less rough and steep; they must be approaching the saddle between the peaks. The wind quickly picked up; the captain felt a fine rain upon his face, and at the same time observed that he was losing grip underfoot. Then he realised that what was falling on him was the greasy rain of Mount Eireaball. He could hear Malachy very close, but still could not see him.

Now the terrain flattened out still further. The wind was coming more strongly over the saddle ahead, and the rain mingled with the swirling mist. He could hear Malachy panting right ahead of him.

"Malachy!" he called into the cloud. "It's no good, Malachy. You've got to come down." The only answer was the incoherent scowl of one past using words, from a man that had been sparing with them at the best of times.

Captain Flaherty inched forward. Suddenly a dark, tall shape appeared in front of him. He stopped in his tracks and his heart missed a beat; then he saw that it was the thorn tree. He edged round it cautiously.

"Malachy!" he cried, hoping to get a bearing on where the man was now. He heard a scowl and stepped towards it; then he saw Malachy right in front of him and made a grab at him. But Malachy pushed him back with force, and the captain staggered back into the tree. He felt the thorns piercing the skin of his head and back through the thickness of his garment, and a trickle of warm blood down his neck. He tried to pull himself out of the bush, but the wool was entangled in it. He pulled harder, wrenched himself free, and made a lunge towards Malachy. This time he succeeded in grabbing an arm, and began to pull on it. As he did so, what the captain did not see was the human form that appeared out of the mist behind him, the figure of the persistent fellow in robes and sandals and tonsured hairstyle, and the weathered face of someone who is at home on the top of a mountain - but now with a wild, mad look of one who has been done serious wrong. And this time his presence was a little less fleeting. Suddenly it seemed to the captain that Malachy smelled of very old fish.

Malachy screamed, and continued to scream into the captain's face; then he began to pull back with a force that could not be resisted, dragging the captain with him. The captain tried to dig his heels in, but there was no grip on the slippery rocks. He felt a strong updraught that he knew must be from the face of the cliff; then the two of them were swaying on the edge of the precipice; and then they were falling. And Malachy was still screaming.

So this was it. There was no further point in holding onto Malachy; and in the same instant the captain remembered that he hadn't uttered St. Scombrel's Invocation; so he did that from beginning to end, very quickly indeed. And so they fell on their separate trajectories, one screaming and the other praying, with equal fervour. So much for all the fancy precautions and spiritual protections.

Just at that moment the heavens opened and there began a long lashing downpour of epic proportions that would rapidly wash away any amount of greasy rain and rehydrate a man in no time at all. But for the captain on his descent it was too much, too late.

28 The Return of the Naïve

As night fell over the island, Dr. O'Toole sat by the fire in his kitchen. He had no idea how many times he'd stepped out the back door and looked out along the bog road, hoping to see a man walking back and dragging another. But it was not to be, and he knew it in his bones. Niamh hadn't come down from her room all day. She hadn't cooked a mackerel. She hadn't done any knitting. She hadn't made a cup of tea. The people of Inishower seemed to know it too. All festival events had been cancelled. At last their spirit was overcome; nobody had the heart for literary affairs at a time like this.

Nonetheless the doctor still waited up, sitting in his high-backed chair and looking out the window that faced the mountain as the night drew on. He thought back over all that had happened since the festival began; and what kept coming back to him were the times he'd had with Flaherty, walking together on the bog road and imparting to him the stories and the lore of Inishower, as you would with a son if you had one; that, of all things, seemed most significant. And yet there was still so much more of the history that he hadn't got round to telling the captain; oddly, that seemed as sad to him now as the rest of the whole sorry mess.

Somewhere in the fitful dozing of the night the doctor awoke from a dream that featured a set of gallows silhouetted against the sky of dawn. The doctor himself was condemning Captain Flaherty to be hanged. Niamh was sobbing at the foot of the gallows, and the people of Inishower stood round in silence; the hangman was Malachy Moodie. Afterwards, as daylight came, the limp body of the captain could be seen hanging from the rope, twisting slowly this way and that in the breeze. The doctor fell again into another troubled sleep.

When he woke once more he was stiff and sore and cold from being in the chair, with the fire gone out. There was a hint of light in the sky. The doctor stared out the window for several minutes before he realised what was wrong: no rain of any kind whatsoever was discernible - a phenomenon that was completely new to him. The sky continued to brighten. Then he heard Niamh come down the stairs and watched her as she entered the kitchen. Her hair was unbrushed and her cheeks streaked with tears. Neither of them spoke. With heavy movements Niamh set about making a new fire in the stove, and then put on a kettle. While it warmed she paced about the room, returning every now and then to look through the window to where the silhouette of the mountain could now be seen with unprecedented clarity.

Now the kettle was boiling, yet Niamh seemed unable to draw herself away from the view. The kettle boiled away. At last she walked back to the stove and warmed the teapot from the kettle. Swilling the water round in the pot, her eyes turned again towards the window. Then she gasped and dropped the teapot; she was halfway towards the door before it shattered on the stone floor. The doctor heard her run down the hall and into the surgery, and in a flash she was back clutching Captain Flaherty's brass telescope. She went straight to the window and focused it on Mount Eireaball. Then she let out a high-pitched cry and was off out the front door towards the village.

Fifteen minutes later Niamh was back with a posse of the stoutest and fiercest knitters, demanding details from the doctor of the pilgrim's route up the mountain, and not taking no for an answer. Half an hour later eight of them strode out on the bog road equipped with offerings, knitting needles and improvised bows to fire them with. By then the rain had come on again.

Three hours after that the group was in the land of mists and on its way up from the cave, winding their way almost to the top. Someone would always keep watch with a bow drawn back, ready to fire if Malachy was seen. When at last a break in the cloud came, Mabel McLintol yelled and pointed up. Seven heads tilted back and saw something dangling from the Cliffs of Manachleim, moving in the wind.

When they reached the top, Niamh stopped. Through the mist she thought she could hear music like some sort of stringed instrument. She moved slowly, inching carefully forward, and found herself walking into St. Scombrel's thorn tree, with the music coming from beyond it. She edged her way round that, and the music grew louder. On the far side of the tree she saw that numerous strands of Inishower wool in familiar shades of blue, green and black ran out over the ground from their entanglement in the branches, stretched tight and with the wind singing over them in unearthly tones. Niamh called three of the women forward to where the stout fibres suddenly dipped down over the edge of the cliff. The four of them lay out on the rock reaching down over the brink, while the other four held onto their legs. They grasped the wool with their stout knitters' fingers, and as they heaved together the muscles stood out on their eight forearms. Then out of the mist steadily rose up the form of Captain Flaherty, stiff as a board and with *scrivlin* and everything else well encrusted with the salt.

Halfway down the mountain, an extended baptism of the disrobed captain in the waters of St. Scombrel's well made short work of his encrustation, and left little doubt in the minds of the other seven women as to the authenticity of his appendage. The captain began to revive. After seven more dunkings in the pools of the Flushey river he was able to walk by himself; and when they got to where the heavy rain was sweeping in over the lowlands he was hardly crackling at all.

The seven knitters of the apocalypse, as they were to go down in history, left Niamh with the captain at the O'Toole abode and set off to find the unfortunate Malachy. They travelled in confident expectation of finding him impaled on the Devil's Quills - a fate which would be judged karmically proper reward for his crimes against knitting. Not that this would prevent him from being ritually *doghtered* as well for good measure, when his lifeless remains would be brought back to the village.

The prizes were duly awarded, the festival resumed, the chemical generation continued to be blithely unaware of anything; and it was widely regarded for decades after as what the doctor had wished for - the best festival ever, even if for mainly extracurricular reasons. Certainly it provided abundant inspiration for the writers of Inishower: and these were decades in which they would be able to tell their wide-eyed children about the day the rain on Inishower *completely stopped.*

And in those decades, visitors to the house where old doctor O'Toole used to live would now find an altogether different kind of man sitting by the fire, writing copious notes on bits of paper that he'd store on shelves in a pantry that had been rebuilt more like a small library, and planning next year's literary festival; and getting a little stiff from time to time when the weather was a bit on the dry side - and an altogether different kind of woman who used to have the worst Cleft on Inishower, knitting for him cardigans and sweaters and socks and gloves and overcoats and hats and scarves and articles for keeping organs warm in winter - and a little girl who'd already developed a fierce habit of hitting little boys round the side of the head with a big wet mackerel.

THE END

Footnote to page 120

Text of a treasured postcard, sent to the author by Seamus Heaney, poet and Nobel Prize winner for literature, upon reading this poem:

"Dear Gerry,

Once upon a time I rhymed 'stirred' with 'word', but now I see that there was another alternative....Thanks for the poem."

www.gerrythompson.co.uk

www.ingramcontent.com/pod-product-compliance
Ingram Content Group UK Ltd.
Pitfield, Milton Keynes, MK11 3LW, UK
UKHW041437180426
11947UKWH00007B/493